CRIME BITERS!

MY DOG IS BETTER THAN YOUR DOG

CRIME BITERS!

MY DOG IS BETTER THAN YOUR DOG

TOMMY GREENWALD
WITH ILLUSTRATIONS BY ADAM STOWER

SCHOLASTIC INC.

ISBN 978-0-545-91669-1

10 9 8 7 6 5 4 3 2 1   15 16 17 18 19

Printed in the U.S.A.   23
First printing 2015

Book design by Yaffa Jaskoll

FOR CATHY UTZ

YEAH, THE HOUSE IS A ZOO.
BUT IT'S *OUR* ZOO.

"Some things are worth fighting for . . . but justice is worth biting for!"
                                        —*Jonah Forrester*

"A crime fighter's job is never done. Catching the bad guys isn't just my job . . . it's my life."
                                        —*Hank Barlow*

INTRODUCTION

PROFILE*

Name: Jimmy Bishop (me)

Age: 11

Occupation: Kid

Interests: Crime fighters, vampires, dogs, not girls

*STOP! POLICE!—which is my all-time-favorite TV show, by the way—does these cool profiles of all the new characters on every episode. So I thought I'd do it too. It's not like I'm stealing the idea or anything. Just paying tribute to it. There's a difference. I think.

I KNOW WHAT YOU'RE THINKING.

You're thinking that just because I love crime fighters, vampires, and dogs, I made up the whole thing about having a crime-fighting vampire dog.

Well, I didn't. It's all true.

Here are three reasons why you know I'm telling the truth.

REASON ONE: First of all, if I was going to invent a crime-fighting vampire dog, do you think I would name her Abby? No. I would name her something totally vampire-ish. Like Hexomitrus.

REASON TWO: If I made up the part about Abby being a crime-fighting vampire dog, why wouldn't I make up the whole rest of the story? Like, why wouldn't I also just say I was the most popular kid in the whole school, a world-champion long-distance runner, and extremely, extremely handsome?

And REASON THREE: This story is so crazy that I don't think *anybody* could have made it up. Not even Elroy Evans, writer of the greatest vampire books ever, or Stanley Murdock, creator of the greatest TV show ever.

So, yeah. What you're about to read is the absolute, exact truth.

I swear!

PART ONE

THE BLOTCH

TUESDAY, AUGUST 26

8:24 A.M.

I'M ONE OF THOSE KIDS WHO LIKES TO STAY busy, because it helps me forget that I don't have a lot to do.

Which makes sense, right?

That's why, on the morning of August 26, I wasn't just eating cereal.

I was also searching for funny dog videos on the computer.

And I was watching YouTube clips of my favorite old TV show—*STOP! POLICE!*

And I was rereading a Jonah Forrester book—*Fang Goodness*—for approximately the six hundred and twenty-eighth time.

In other words, Tuesday, August 26, was a typical summer morning, until my sister, Misty, walked into the kitchen, looked at me, and dropped her phone.

"EW!" she screamed. "Jimmy, you have a huge blotch on your face!"

FACT: There's never a good time for a blotch to suddenly appear on your face, but some times are worse than others. And 8:24 in the morning, two days before the first day of fifth grade, is probably just about the worst time of all.

By the way, I had no idea what a blotch was.

"What's a blotch?" I asked Misty.

"A big, disgusting, gross mark!" she explained happily.

PROFILE
Name: Misty Bishop (sister)
Age: 14
Occupation: Texting
Interests: The usual annoying big-sister things

All of a sudden, a feeling of panic filled my chest.

"MOM!" I called. But then I remembered she wasn't home, as usual. She left really early for work every day, and came home late too.

"DAD!"

My dad, who was in the TV room, came in and took a look.

"Wow," he said, "she's a beaut." He leaned in closer. "And if I'm not mistaken," he added, "it's the exact shape of Rhode Island." Then his phone buzzed. "Sorry, bud, I gotta deal with this."

I ran to the bathroom and stared at myself in the mirror.

Ugh.

I had no idea what Rhode Island looked like, but it had to be the ugliest state in the entire country.

I stood there for about five seconds. Then I did what any kid who discovers a Rhode Island–shaped blotch on his face, two days before fifth grade, would do.

I screamed.

"NOOOOOOOOOO!"

My sister poked her head in. "YEESSSSSSSSS!" she said, cracking up.

FACT: When your older sister looks at you and starts laughing, you know it's not good.

8:47 A.M.

I WAS STILL STARING AT MYSELF IN THE BATHROOM MIRROR, wishing there was a hole in the wall I could crawl into, when my dad walked in with a huge smile on his face.

"Good news—I got the interview!" he announced. "I just called Mom. I've got to be in the city in an hour and a half. Your sister will keep an eye on you today." He scooped me up in his arms and started dancing and singing a made-up song. "We're gonna need a babysitter all up in here, 'cause your dad's finally getting things in gear!" I tried to be patient because I knew how badly my dad needed some good news—he'd been looking for a job for almost a year—but after a few more seconds, I decided patience was overrated.

"Dad!" I whined. "Stop!"

When he realized how upset I was, he put me down and tried to act upset too, which was like an elephant trying to act small.

"Oh, that thing on your face isn't so bad," he said. "It's probably just nerves, a rash of some sort, since school starts in a couple of days. I bet it will be gone by tonight."

"But what if it's not?" I said, starting to cry.

My dad looked nervous. I think he was trying to figure out how to deal with a crying son, while not being late for his interview.

"Um . . . uh . . . C'mon, Jimmy . . ."

"YOU NEED TO STAY HERE TODAY AND HELP ME GET RID OF MY BLOTCH!" I wailed. "MOM'S NOT HERE! YOU NEED TO STAY!"

Then, all of a sudden, out of nowhere, he said the one thing he knew would calm me down.

"Listen, hey, maybe we should think about getting that dog after all. How about it? Whaddya say?"

I stopped crying.

FACT: It's amazing how fast you can stop crying when you hear something that makes you a lot less sad than you were three seconds earlier.

ANOTHER FACT: I should probably mention that I've asked my parents for a dog approximately 3,593 times in my life, and every time, they'd always say the same thing:

"Now's not a good time."

WELL . . . as it turned out, throwing a tantrum because there's a gross mark on your face, while your dad is trying to leave so he can get hired for a job, is a really good time.

"For real? A dog?" I puffed out my cheeks so my blotch seemed even bigger. "But what about you and Mom saying it's too much work and everyone's too busy and Mom not wanting her rugs to get ruined and all that other stuff you always bring up when I ask for a dog?"

My dad sighed. For a minute I thought he was going to take it back, but he didn't. "Yeah, well, we'll figure it out. When I get back from the city, we'll go to the shelter."

"When will you be back?"

"A few hours. But I have to leave now. Deal?"

"Deal!" I hugged my dad. He hugged me back, then said, "Gotta go," and ran out the door.

I stood there, staring at my blotch in the mirror. Suddenly, it didn't look that horrible.

Don't get me wrong, it still looked horrible.

Just not *that* horrible.

10:13 A.M.

MY MOM CALLED, and we had pretty much our usual conversation—with a few new twists.

"Hi, honey. What are you doing?"

"Not much."

"What's your sister doing?"

"I don't know."

"Are you outside?"

"No."

"Why not? It's a beautiful day."

"I don't feel like it."

"Go outside, Jimmy."

"If you really cared about me being outside, you'd be here to make sure I went outside."

"Jimmy, you're being ridiculous. You know I have to work. Stop trying to make me feel guilty about it."

"I'm not trying to make you feel guilty about it."

PROFILE

Name: Richard Bishop (father)

Age: I forget exactly

Occupation: Taking care of my sister and me

Interests: Finding a job so he doesn't have to take care of my sister and me anymore

A brief pause as we try to not get in a fight.

"Fine. So what are you doing?"

"Nothing."

"Are you watching *STOP! POLICE!?*"

"Maybe."

"Stop watching so much TV."

"It's a really good episode."

"You need to be with people."

"I don't really like that many people."

"What about Irwin? Why don't you invite Irwin over?"

"Maybe later."

"Well, you need to get out and get some fresh air."

"I will, Mom. Hey, did you hear? We're getting a dog!"

(New twist.)

"I heard. Dad told me."

"Isn't that awesome?"

"I guess."

"You don't sound like you think it's awesome."

"Well, I admit I was a little surprised, he should have asked me first. That's generally how it's done. But I guess it's time. It will be good for you. You need something like this. But you're going to need to be the one to take care of it."

PROFILE

Name: Sarah Bishop (mother)

Age: She'd rather not talk about it

Occupation: Something that involves a big briefcase

Interests: Whatever is inside that big briefcase

"I will."

"We'll see. Your father will help too, since this whole thing was his idea."

"I think it's because he felt sorry for me because I have a thing on my face. Misty called it a blotch." *(Another new twist.)*

"Right. I heard about that too. I'll take a look tonight."

"And also since you're never home and he might get a job, Dad probably thought I needed a pal."

"Stop trying to make me feel guilty, honey."

"The blotch better go away before school, Mom."

"Oh, I'm sure it will. We'll talk later; I'm late for a meeting. Love you."

"Next time you see me we'll have a dog." *(Last new twist.)*

"We'll see. Bye."

"Bye."

12:39 P.M.

"EEEWWW!" IRWIN WONK SAID, POINTING AT MY FACE AS WE SAT ON THE SWING SET THAT WE WERE WAY TOO OLD FOR.

Irwin and I have been friends ever since kindergarten, after discovering that we both liked to use potato chips to scrape the ice cream off our ice-cream sandwiches. He was a pretty good kid, and we went over to each other's houses a lot. One day we decided to be best friends. I guess because "best friend" sounds better than "only friend."

But that was before I had a big blotch on my face.

"I'm not sure I can be best friends with you anymore," Irwin went on. "I mean, look at that thing."

"First of all, it's called a blotch," I told him. And second of all, I feel lousy enough without you being all mean about it. Why don't you and your lisp go somewhere else?"

PROFILE

Name: Irwin Wonk (best friend)

Age: 11

Occupation: Talking too much

Interests: Picking his nose when he thinks no one is looking

Irwin looked hurt, and even though he had insulted me first, I felt a little guilty. He had a pretty bad lisp, which he was embarrassed about. Secretly I liked his lisp though, because it sounded really weird—and also because it meant he was less likely to find some other kid to be best friends with.

"I'll take it back if you take it back," I added.

He thought for a second, then nodded. "Okay, deal. Let's talk about something else. Let's talk about Daisy."

My heart immediately made a weird somersault.

Daisy Flowers.

Daisy Flowers.

Daaaaiiissssy Fffflllllooowwweeeersssss.

FACT: You can tell what a girl is like from her name.

Daisy had moved into the house directly across from mine at the beginning of the summer, and ever since then, Irwin and I had talked a lot *about* her. But we were both way too scared to actually talk *to* her. We didn't really talk to *any* girls, especially ones named Daisy Flowers.

"You totally like Daisy," Irwin said.

"I totally do not!" I said back. "You totally like Daisy!"

"That's a lie!"

We sat there, glaring at each other.

The truth was, Irwin and I *both* liked Daisy Flowers.

"Let's go over to her house and see if she wants to hang out," Irwin suggested.

"Maybe later," I said.

Irwin stomped his foot. "Not later; now! You guys are friends! I want to be friends too!"

"We're not friends," I corrected.

"You totally are," he insisted.

"We had one conversation."

"That's one more than I've had!"

I sighed. Irwin was really jealous of that conversation, even though it had lasted exactly eight seconds. One day, when I was outside reading, Daisy came out of her house. She noticed me, stopped, and actually walked over.

"What are you reading?" she'd asked.

"*Fangs for the Memories* by Elroy Evans," I'd told her. "Jonah Forrester gets amnesia and forgets he's a vampire, until he bites the nurse who's taking care of him. But then he remembers and saves all the patients from an evil doctor who's taking their kidneys and selling them."

PROFILE
Name: Daisy Flowers (neighbor)
Age: A perfect 10
Occupation: Being perfect
Interests: Perfection

"That sounds good," Daisy had said. "Gross, but good. Well, gotta go."

"Okay, bye," I'd said.

Later, when I told Irwin about it, he got really mad. He thought Daisy and I had decided to be friends without him. He wanted to be friends with her too, and he'd been really annoying about it ever since.

"Well, I don't care what you do, I'm going over to her house," Irwin was saying now.

"Yeah, right."

"Yeah, right, yourself."

I tried to change the subject. "What kind of dog do you think I should get? Do you want to come over tonight and meet him?"

Irwin shrugged. "Sure. Maybe I'll come over for dinner or something." He loved our selection of ice cream and cookies. It was one of the side benefits of having a dad home to do the shopping instead of a mom.

"Did you know Hank Barlow has a cool police dog named Justice?" I asked Irwin. "I think he's a German shepherd. Jonah Forrester doesn't have a dog, but I bet if he did it would be a Doberman pinscher or something like that."

Irwin rolled his eyes. "What is it with you and Hank Barlow, and those stupid Jonah Forrester books? That police show is like a hundred years old, and vampires aren't even real. And that's cool that you're getting a dog, but it's dumb to talk about what kind, because you're just going to go to the shelter and get whatever's available." He glanced back toward Daisy's house. "Come on, let's go over."

I was in the middle of deciding whether to yell at him because of his dumb idea to go to Daisy's house, or yell at him because of his mean insults about Hank Barlow and Jonah Forrester, when Misty stuck her head out the front door.

"Lunch, brats!" she hollered. Whenever Misty had to babysit me, she was the worst person alive. I think it was because since she hated doing it, she wanted to make sure I was just as miserable as she was.

"Great!" I exclaimed, happy that Misty had saved me from a possibly really embarrassing situation. We were just getting ready to go inside when we heard a noise from across the street.

The sound of Daisy's front door.

Sure enough, out she came, dressed in a bathing suit.

A few seconds later, her mom followed, carrying some towels.

We stared.

"I wonder where they're going," Irwin said.

"Maybe swimming," I said.

"You two are pathetic," Misty said.

Daisy started walking to her car, but before she got in, she looked over at us and gave us a wave.

That was all Irwin needed, and he broke into a huge smile. "See, I told you! I knew she liked me! Excellent!"

Just between you and me? When he said *excellent*, it sounded more like *ekthellent*.

4:16 P.M.

SO MY DAD'S VERSION OF GETTING HOME "IN A FEW HOURS" WAS BASICALLY EIGHT HOURS LATER.

I waited by the front door, trying to stay calm.

It didn't work.

"WHERE'S DAD?" I screamed at Misty, who was blasting music while combing her hair for the sixty-second time that day.

"HOW SHOULD I KNOW?" she screamed back, turning up the music.

"I HATE YOU!" I screamed louder.

"I HATE YOU MORE!" she screamed loudest.

It was kind of a routine we had.

4:56 P.M.

FINALLY, DAD PULLED INTO THE DRIVEWAY, HONKING HIS HORN.

"Get in! We're late."

We're late?!? WE?!?!

"Where were you?" I asked, but I could tell he was totally distracted. "Dad! Stop staring at your phone!"

"I'm waiting for an important call," he said, which I guess was his version of an apology.

FACT: Dads are horrible at apologizing.

"About the job?" I asked.

"Yeah."

On the way to the shelter neither of us talked for a few minutes. I could tell he was nervous.

"So can I get any dog I want?" I asked.

28

"Sure," said my dad. "As long as it's between fourteen and nineteen months old, and weighs between twenty-five and thirty-five pounds."

"That's not exactly *any* dog, Dad," I grumbled, as the GPS lady told us to take a left.

"Mom talked to somebody at work who's a big-time animal lover," Dad said. "She says we should get a dog who's past the crazy puppy phase but still young enough to be fun and playful. And size-wise, I don't want one of those tiny, fluffy dogs that movie stars put in their pocketbooks, but I also don't want one of those monster dogs that takes up the entire couch."

Those ground rules sounded a little strict to me. What if I wanted to get a dog that was thirty-seven pounds?

"But, Dad—"

"No buts."

He turned the radio on and started drumming on the steering wheel. Conversation officially over.

WHEN I WALKED IN TO THE NORTHPORT ANIMAL RESCUE FOUNDATION (OTHERWISE KNOWN AS NORTHPORT ARF!), dogs and cats of all shapes and sizes tried to get my attention. It was like a kickball game and I was the captain, and they were all yelling, "PICK ME! PICK ME!" But it wasn't a kickball game. It was real life, and they all wanted me to take them home so they could feel safe and warm and loved.

"Look!" I yelled. "They're so cute! I want all of them!"

Even my dad, who was staring at his phone waiting for it to ring, seemed to be affected by all the cuteness. He actually smiled a few times. But he shook his head. "Nice try, Jimmy. You know the deal. One dog." He pointed at a beagle that was jumping in circles. "And nothing too crazy. We don't want our house ripped to shreds."

FACT: If you consider yourself not that popular of a person, go to an animal shelter. You will feel really popular, really fast.

I noticed a cocker spaniel that was wagging its tail and barking. "How about that one?"

My dad shook his head again. "I'm not sure I can listen to that barking all night. And the neighbors would hate us."

I soon discovered that my dad had a reason to turn down pretty much every dog I pointed at or played with.

"Too big."

"Too small."

"Too hairy." "Too smelly." "Too loud." "Too sleepy." "Too young." "Too playful."

My dad was "too annoying."

I knew it. This whole thing was a setup. He'd said we would get a dog only so I would stop whining about my blotch and he could go to his stupid interview. (The blotch was still there, by the way, in case you were wondering.)

I was about to give up, when we rounded the last corner of the last room in the whole place and saw this dark tiny cage in the corner. All I could see were two bright lights shining straight at me. As I walked closer, I realized they weren't lights at all. They were eyes.

I ran over to the cage and looked in. There was a scruffy little dog, just lying there. He looked like a combination of a thousand different breeds—he had spots, he had stripes, his eyes were two different colors, his ears were two different shapes, and he had a big black streak of fur right down his back, almost like a cape. He was wagging his tail sleepily, and he had the cutest, saddest face I'd ever seen.

In other words, he was *awesome*.

I ran over to one of the guys who worked there. "Hi! Is this dog available? Is he nice?"

The guy nodded. "Oh, she's a bit of a loner. Likes to sleep all day, but she's wide-awake at night. The doc thinks her eyes are supersensitive to light for some reason. A total sweetheart though."

Oh! So he was a she. Hmmm. I'd always imagined having a boy dog. Oh well.

"How old is she?"

"About a year and a half."

"How much does she weigh?"

The guy scratched his head. "What is this, the third degree? I'd say about thirty pounds."

Yes! Perfect.

"Dad! I found her! I found her!"

Dad was still messing around with his phone. "Oh yeah?"

"Come quick!"

He sighed and walked over to the cage to take a look. After about a minute, he asked the worker guy, "Can you please take her out so we can say hi?"

The guy opened the cage and brought the dog over. As I started petting her, she looked right into my eyes. I could swear she was smiling! She seemed sleepy, but she was soooooo cute! She didn't look like any dog I'd ever seen before.

"What kind of dog is she?" I asked.

"A whole lot of everything," said the guy.

"What's her name?"

The guy laughed. "Whatever you want it to be."

"Let me take a look," my dad said. The guy handed him the-dog-with-no-name. My dad stood there for a few seconds, just kind of staring at her. He didn't look very enthusiastic. In fact, he looked like he was reconsidering the whole thing. I started to think this whole dog thing would never happen.

All of a sudden, the dog stretched, pulled her head back, and sneezed right in my dad's face.

That's right. You heard me.

FACT: If you're in the middle of adopting a dog, try to make sure it doesn't sneeze in your dad's face.

"BLECH!" my dad said. He scowled as he handed the dog to me, while the worker guy tried not to laugh.

"Dad?" I said, but I knew it was over. There was no way we were getting this dog.

Then my dad's phone rang.

He looked at the phone. Then he looked at me.

"You better get it," I said.

As my dad walked off down the hall, I waited there with the dog still in my hands. She was pretty heavy, so I sat down on the floor. "Why did you have to sneeze right then?" I asked her, but she wouldn't answer.

Finally, after three or four long minutes, my dad came back. His eyes were sparkling.

"Looks like I got a good shot," he said, giving me a big hug. "They want me to come back in tomorrow afternoon to meet some other people. They say I'm the leading candidate."

"That's great, Dad!"

He bent down and stared into the dog's eyes. "Hey, maybe you're a good-luck charm after all."

Then my dad looked at the guy who worked there.

"We'll take her."

My heart did a somersault. I couldn't believe it! I was getting a dog! Finally!

I gave the dog a big bear hug—or I guess, a dog hug—and when she licked me back, I was pretty sure she winked at me.

That was the moment I first started wondering if she had secret powers.

5:33 P.M.

HOW ABBY BECAME ABBY:

My dad had to do a bunch of paperwork for the shelter before we could take our new dog home.

At the same time, he was talking on the phone to my mom, and e-mailing the people who were setting up his next interview.

"They want a name," he said to me.

"Jimmy Bishop," I told him.

Dad rolled his eyes. "For the dog."

"Oh."

FACT: Sometimes kids get dumber in front of their parents.

I looked at the dog. The dog looked back at me. She had the cutest face I'd ever seen, but also the saddest. I wanted to name her something that would make her a little less sad.

"Happy," I said to my dad. "Let's name her Happy."

"Got it," he said. I wasn't sure if he was saying that to me or to my mom on the phone. Then he wrote something down and handed the paperwork to the lady who ran the shelter.

"Congratulations," she said. "Getting a dog is a wonderful thing, both for your family and your pet." She looked down at the paperwork. "Abby is a very lucky girl."

Huh?

I stared at my dad. "Abby?"

He stared back. "What? That's what you said."

I looked at the dog, who had been named Happy for about seven seconds. But you know what? I didn't care what her name was. As long as she was mine.

"Hi, Abby," I said. "I'm Jimmy."

6:17 P.M.

WHEN WE GOT BACK TO THE HOUSE, there was a strange car in the driveway.

"Who's that, Dad?"

Dad turned off the engine. "Must be the new sitter."

"New sitter? What happened to Becky?" I loved Becky. She was nice and friendly and always let me have seconds for dessert.

"She had to go back to college," my dad said. "I know you wish she was your full-time babysitter, but it turns out she has other career goals."

"That stinks. Why tonight?"

Dad sighed. "While we were getting Abby, Mom called to remind me that she has a client in town, and I'm supposed to join them for dinner."

"But we just got a new dog!"

"Yeah, no kidding," said my dad. "Great timing, huh?

I'm pretty sure your mother's not too happy with me right about now."

"Whatever." I couldn't care less if Mom was mad at Dad. It was her fault that she was always busy. Meanwhile, I had a new dog and a new babysitter, all on the same night. I suddenly got a nervous feeling in my stomach.

While my dad checked his phone for the ninety-ninth time that day, I put the leash on Abby to go inside. I had to wake her up—she'd slept the whole way home, which was kind of amazing, since I figured she'd be super excited about her new adventure.

I guess she was *kind of* excited though—because the minute we got in the house, she peed on the floor.

"Well, well, well," said a voice I'd never heard before. "What have we here? Let's get that cleaned up!"

I looked up and saw a lady walking in from the kitchen with a mop, smiling down at my brand-new dog. The lady was very tall, and she walked with a cane. Everything about her seemed kind of old except for her hair—she had long red hair.

The lady looked at me. "Hello there," she said.

"Are you the new babysitter?"

She smiled, revealing a mouthful of jagged, yellow teeth.

PROFILE

Name: Mrs. Cragg

Age: Not sure I can count that high

Occupation: Babysitter

Interests: Not brushing her teeth, apparently

"I am indeed, young man. And you must be Jimmy."

She seemed friendly enough, but I noticed she was looking at my blotch. Suddenly, I felt nervous.

"I—I—"

Before I could spit it out, my dad came through the front door. "Ah, Mrs. Cragg," he said. "So nice to meet you. My wife mentioned you'd be here."

Mrs. Cragg? What kind of a name is that?

"I am indeed Mrs. Cragg," she answered, running her hand through her hair. "And you must be Mr. Bishop! A real pleasure to meet you."

As they shook hands, Mrs. Cragg looked down at Abby. "I didn't realize a dog was part of the equation," she said. Abby looked up at the lady and yawned.

"Oh, yes," said my dad. "One of those spontaneous decisions, I'm afraid. Hopefully that's not a problem?"

"Not at all," said the old lady, but I could tell by her eyes she was lying.

My dad turned to me. "Jimmy, with Becky going back to college, and me hopefully going back to work, we thought it might be a good time to get some more permanent help. Someone who can take care of you after school, and drive you and your sister to activities, that kind of thing. And since Mom and I need to go out to dinner tonight, we thought we'd get a head start on things." He nodded at Mrs. Cragg. "Mom ended up calling *Barnaby Bratford's Bestest Babysitters* and asked Mr. Bratford for his most highly regarded employee, and he sent over Mrs. Cragg. If everything works out tonight, she'll come back tomorrow afternoon while I'm in the city. Sound good?"

Dad held his hand out for a high five, but I was too busy staring at Mrs. Cragg. She gave me and my dad a warm smile—but when she looked at the dog, the smile disappeared.

I looked at Abby. She wasn't yawning anymore. Now she was totally alert, staring back up at Mrs. Cragg.

A standoff.

Uh-oh, I thought to myself.

This can't be good.

6:42 P.M.

WHEN MISTY GOT HOME FROM CHEERLEADING PRAC-TICE, I was in my room, putting up a new Hank Barlow poster. She came upstairs, took one look at Abby, and started laughing.

"What kind of a ridiculous-looking dog is *that*?!?"

Have I mentioned that Misty is a terrible, horrible person?

"The best kind," I snapped. "The kind that needed to be rescued."

Misty bent down to get a closer look. "Well, I guess she's so ugly, she's cute." She petted Abby for a few seconds, then stared down at her hand. "Ew! Dog fur!" she screamed, and ran to the bathroom.

FACT: Even though a brother and sister might have the same parents, it's still possible for them to be the two most opposite people who have ever lived.

After scrubbing Abby's fur off her like it was chicken pox or something, Misty came back into my room and flopped down on my bed. "What's the deal with the new babysitter?" she said. "Mrs. Cragg? What kind of a name is that?"

I nodded. "Beats me. Dad said that Becky went back to college."

"Bummer," said Misty. "For you, I mean." Since Misty was fourteen, she didn't consider herself part of the whole babysitter situation—although she liked having one, because it meant she could go out whenever she wanted and not have to watch me.

"Gee, thanks," I said. "I'm already pretty sure that Abby and Mrs. Cragg don't like each other."

Misty rolled her eyes. "Whatever. I just hope Dad doesn't get that job."

"That's a terrible thing to say!" I said. But I secretly agreed with her. Having Dad home was awesome.

Misty's phone buzzed. She read a text, laughed, and immediately texted back.

"What was that?" I asked her.

"Just friend stuff," she said. She said that to me all the time. *Just friend stuff.* Translation: *Stop being such a nosy little brother.*

Misty got up. "Okay, enough chitty chat." She headed toward her room, where she would spend the next three hours texting her friends, listening to music, and combing her hair. But two minutes later, she popped her head back in.

"Oh, and by the way, your blotch is bigger."

ACK! My blotch!

It was my turn to freak out and run to the bathroom. I stared in the mirror. She was right—it *was* bigger. A lot bigger! My blotch had expanded like an inch on all sides! I remembered my dad had said it looked like Rhode Island, and when I looked up Rhode Island, I found out it was the smallest state in the country. Oh no! What if it kept growing until it went through all fifty states? What if it became California or Texas or Alaska by the time school started?

I decided I might have to skip school this year.

7:09 P.M.

WHEN MY MOM FINALLY GOT HOME A LITTLE AFTER SEVEN, I ran downstairs to show her my blotch and Abby. But Mrs. Cragg was already waiting at the door, smiling brightly.

"Hello, I'm Mrs. Cragg," she said, all her jagged yellow teeth showing.

"A pleasure to meet you," said my mom, as they shook hands. Then she saw me, waiting in the hall. "There he is," Mom said, as she scooped me up in her arms (my parents were big on the scooping). "Let me see this tiny little mark everyone's so worried about." She examined my face. "Oh, that's nothing!"

"It's not a mark, it's a blotch," I said. "And it's not nothing, Mom. It's horrible, and it's getting bigger. If you were home more, instead of working all the time and going out to dinner with clients, you'd know that."

"Don't you start with me," she said, kissing the tip of my nose. "We'll get some medicine to take care of it. And at least you got a dog as part of the deal! Where is the little lady anyway?"

I grabbed my mom's hand and took her to the closet, where Abby was snoozing on top of some shoes. As my mom bent down to pet her, Abby woke up, licked my mom's hand, and went back to sleep.

"She is adorable!" Mom said. "And so well-behaved."

"I know!" I said. "But she sleeps a lot. I hope she wants to play soon."

"Oh, I'm sure she will." My mom stood up, took off her shoes, and sighed happily. "Taking off these heels is one of the highlights of my day. Too bad I have to put them back on in twenty minutes. Is Misty home? And where's Dad? He's coming to this dinner with me, whether he likes it or not."

I tried not to look too grumpy. "I think he's taking a shower or something."

"Don't you worry, we'll bring dessert back just for you," Mom said, knowing I was grumpy anyway.

FACT: Moms are good at reading their kids' minds.

"Chocolate coconut cake?" I asked.

My mom smiled. "With double frosting."

ANOTHER FACT: Double frosting may be the two best words in the English language.

"Okay," I said. I was just about to add *Could you get a little extra piece for Abby?* when Dad came downstairs, carrying my mom's favorite necklace. "This ought to impress your client," he said. "It's almost as beautiful as you are."

"Hmmm," my mom said. "As if one little compliment would make me forget that you got a dog without asking me."

"How about two little compliments?" said my dad. "I missed you so much today."

She kissed him and laughed. "Now you're getting somewhere."

Mrs. Cragg stared at the necklace. "That is truly magnificent," she said. "Such beautiful diamonds!"

"You're telling me," said my dad. "I bought it in a moment of madness, back when I thought I could afford it."

Mrs. Cragg's eyes were still on the necklace. "Well, you have terrific taste. It looks simply spectacular on your lovely wife."

My mom blushed.

"Well, gotta go," said my dad. "Remember, Jimmy, only one episode of *STOP! POLICE!* tonight."

"I'll make sure," Mrs. Cragg said, before I could answer. "Too much television is bad for you."

Ugh.

Double frosting wasn't going to be enough.

Better make it triple.

7:47 P.M.

THEN A STRANGE THING HAPPENED.

After my parents left, and it got darker out, Abby got a lot less tired and a lot more playful.

It started when Irwin came over for dinner around seven thirty. Abby sprang out of the closet, jumped up, and started kissing him all over his face.

"He's so hyper!" Irwin said, trying to catch his breath. "Holy moly!"

"He's a she," I corrected him, wondering a little jealously why Abby hadn't yet welcomed me the same way. "Here, girl!" I said. Abby turned, then jumped on me and started kissing me, while wagging her tail like crazy.

"I thought she was kind of lazy, but I guess not!" I said, relieved.

It turned out she was just getting warmed up. At dinner, after Abby finished her dog food, she picked up the bowl and ran all over the house with it.

Mrs. Cragg didn't like that at all. "STOP THAT DOG! STOP THAT DOG!" she kept yelling.

Abby basically just laughed at her and kept going.

It was awesome.

FACT: In a contest between an adorable dog and an annoyed babysitter, it's pretty easy to know who to root for.

Mrs. Cragg started chasing Abby around with her cane in one hand and a big wooden spoon in the other. Abby turned around, grabbed the spoon out of Mrs. Cragg's hand, and turned that into a toy too.

"GIVE ME BACK MY SPOON!" Mrs. Cragg hollered.

As if.

Misty came out of her room. "Jimmy, calm that dog down!" she ordered. "I'm trying to do my summer reading!" By which she meant, reading texts from her friends about what color lipstick they wanted to try next.

Finally, Abby dropped the two kitchen utensils. Then she ran to the front door and started barking like crazy.

"I think she wants to go out," Irwin said.

"Wow, you're a genius," I told him.

"Well, you're the opposite of a genius," he told me back.

I put the leash on Abby. "My parents said we could take Abby out if we kept her in the yard the whole time," I called out to Mrs. Cragg, who was doing dishes in the kitchen. "Be back in a few minutes!"

"Fine," she yelled back. I think she would have been happier if I said a few *hours*.

The minute we got outside, Abby started pulling on the leash like crazy. Soon, she was dragging me all over the yard.

"She's strong for her size," Irwin observed. I resisted the temptation to call him a genius again.

"Easy, Abby!" I said. "Slow down!"

"Woof!" she said back, which I think meant, *I'm going to pretend I don't understand what you're asking me.*

She pulled harder.

It was pretty dark by now, but we had the outside lights on, so I could see what she was pulling me toward— a small hole at the edge of the yard, where some creature probably lived. Abby stuck her nose down the hole and started digging and barking. I felt really sorry for the creature down there. It was probably scared out of its wits.

Or not.

Because the creature turned out to be a groundhog, and all of a sudden it popped its head up and made this weird angry noise, like, *Get off my property!*

Well, Abby didn't like that. She didn't like that *at all.* She lunged forward and growled.

And when she growled, I saw her fangs for the first time.

WHOA.

I always knew dogs had fangs, but these fangs were capital letter FANGS. They were HUGE. And SHARP. And SERIOUS.

Practically Jonah Forrester fangs.

The groundhog must have thought so too, because it went back down its hole in about half a second and never came back up. Abby kept growling though.

"*Abby!*" I said. "That's enough!"

She finally put her fangs away, looked up at me, and wagged her tail. Then she jumped up and gave me a huge kiss!

"We better go back inside," Irwin said. I think he was a little surprised by Abby's unpredictable behavior.

He wasn't the only one.

8:19 P.M.

IRWIN AND I PLAYED WITH ABBY FOR ANOTHER HALF HOUR. She still had tons of energy. Even though we'd gotten a bunch of dog toys from the shelter, she preferred playing with an empty milk container that she stole from the recycling bin.

FACT: Dogs like playing with non-toys more than toys.

When Mrs. Cragg tried to take the milk container away, out came Abby's fangs.

"This dog is insane!" screamed Mrs. Cragg.

Irwin and I laughed.

"It's not funny!" bellowed Mrs. Cragg.

She was wrong.

Abby kept driving Mrs. Cragg crazy until nine o'clock, when Irwin's dad came to pick him up. Meanwhile, I was getting tired, my parents weren't home yet, and Abby was still running all over the house.

I texted my dad: ABBY IS ACTING KIND OF HYPER. WHAT KIND OF DOG IS SHE?

Five minutes later, he texted me back: HOME IN TWENTY MINUTES. MAKE SURE SHE DOESN'T BREAK ANYTHING.

Not helpful.

I knocked on my sister's door. She opened it a crack.

"What do you want?"

"Abby's being really weird. She slept all day but now it's nighttime and she's got tons of energy. Plus her fangs are huge."

Misty rolled her eyes. "What is wrong with you? Newsflash: dogs sleep a lot. And double newsflash: dogs have fangs."

She shut her door with a SLAM.

I played tug-of-war with Abby and the milk container in the TV room for a while more, until Mrs. Cragg yelled from the kitchen, "Jimmy, time to get ready for bed!" I guess her new policy was to not be in any room that Abby was in.

When I went to the bathroom to brush my teeth, I looked in the mirror.

I couldn't believe it.

My facial blotch was *smaller*!

It turned out playing with Abby while she made Mrs. Cragg miserable was the best thing that could have happened to my blotch!

A few minutes later, my parents got home, and I gobbled down my chocolate coconut cake in about three bites. As my parents talked to Mrs. Cragg, she smiled at them as if everything was totally swell. "We had a wonderful evening," she said, twirling her bright red hair. "Your children are so well-behaved, and that little dog is just adorable."

Misty, who had come downstairs to watch TV in the other room, looked up at me and rolled her eyes.

My mom asked me, "Honey, did you and Irwin have a good time tonight?"

I was about to say that Mrs. Cragg and Abby didn't get along, but then I got this bad feeling that my parents would blame the strange new dog instead of the sweet old lady. I didn't want to risk any bad feelings about Abby. Not on the first day.

"Everything was great," I said. "And we didn't watch TV the whole time."

My mom pretended to faint. "It's a miracle!"

My dad shook Mrs. Cragg's hand. "Well, so far so good," my dad told her. "What do you say we give this a shot? I have to be back in the city for more interviews over the next few days. Would you mind coming in the afternoons for the rest of the week?"

"Seriously?" Misty yelled from the other room.

"Not for you," my mom said. "For Jimmy."

Mrs. Cragg smiled at my parents. "I'd be delighted," she said. "In the meantime, I've made some breakfast treats for you to enjoy in the morning. They're in the fridge."

I looked at Abby. She looked at me. I'm pretty sure we were both thinking the same thing:

We better get used to looking at yellow teeth.

10:09 P.M.

I ASKED DAD TO LET ABBY SLEEP IN MY ROOM.

He yawned. "Fine."

FACT: The best time to ask your parents for something is when they're really tired.

I hopped into bed and picked up my copy of *Fang Goodness*, my favorite book of all time. Did I mention that already? Anyway, *Fang Goodness* is the first book in the Jonah Forrester series, the one where Jonah discovers he's a vampire. But Jonah decides to use his powers for good, so he becomes a policeman in Los Angeles, where no one knows his true identity. I was rereading the part where he goes to a Los Angeles Dodgers game and saves everyone by biting a bad guy who is about to fill the concession stands with poisonous hot dogs.

Jonah Forrester is awesome. Vampires are awesome.

I think the last thing I thought before falling asleep was, *I hope I meet a vampire one day.*

SOMETIME AFTER 12:00 A.M.

I REMEMBER DREAMING ABOUT JONAH FORRESTER TAKING ME OUT FOR ICE CREAM AND HIM ORDERING A STRAWBERRY MILK SHAKE.

I remember hearing a *whoosh!*, like the wind, and then a *thwack!*, like a door slam.

I remember rubbing my eyes and looking around.

I remember checking Abby's bed and realizing that she wasn't there.

I remember noticing that the window was open.

I remember looking out the window and seeing a small shape scurrying along the driveway.

I remember thinking it was Abby but then saying to myself, *You're half-asleep, you're probably just seeing things.*

I remember lying back down in bed, thinking about stuff. How I had a blotch on my face. How I got an awesome but strange dog. How I got a new babysitter. How Dad might get a job.

And I remember the last thing I said to myself before I fell back asleep: *Boy, what a crazy day.*

I had no idea the craziness was just getting started.

PART TWO

THE BULLY

WEDNESDAY, AUGUST 27

8:33 A.M.

BLOTCH REPORT: SEEMS TO HAVE GOTTEN WORSE OVERNIGHT. Dad reports it now looks like North Dakota. I looked up North Dakota. It's the seventeenth biggest state in the country. Only sixteen more to go.

Oh, and tomorrow's the first day of school.

Yay.

As soon as I woke up, I checked Abby's bed. She wasn't there! But then, for some reason, I looked in the closet and there she was, sleeping peacefully, buried in the dirty clothes I'd shoved in the corner.

I suddenly had this random thought: *Jonah Forrester sleeps in his closet.*

Hmmmm.

I tried to wake Abby up, but she just looked at me, wagged her tail for a second, then went back to sleep. I looked over at the window. It was open. Slowly the whole semi-dream thing came back to me.

Did Abby really go out in the middle of the night?

Like Jonah Forrester does?

Okay, I thought to myself. *That's enough of that.*

I headed downstairs for breakfast. Mom was already gone, as usual. Misty was still sleeping. She liked to sleep a lot during the summer. (I couldn't wait to see her get up at six fifteen tomorrow for school—that was going be *fun*.)

Meanwhile, Dad was looking at himself in the hall mirror, deciding which tie to wear for his big interview later that day. He tried on about twenty before settling on a blue one with purple flowers on it.

"Whaddya think?" he asked me.

"I think it's totally spectacular," I answered. "I think it's the best tie ever and you'll not only get the job but also get a raise and a promotion." I stood next to him in front of the mirror. "Meanwhile, my blotch is also blue and purple, so we have that in common."

"Now, come on," Dad said. "Mom is bringing some medicine home tonight and that thing will be gone by morning. Just you wait."

"What is that gross smell?" I said, changing the subject.

"Ah, yes," said my dad. "Those are Mrs. Cragg's breakfast goodies. Let's go take a look. She's going to get you and me off all our sugary treats and onto a healthy diet. Isn't that great?"

"No, it's the opposite of great."

When we walked into the kitchen, I had to hold my nose. It smelled like old socks soaked in swamp juice.

"What *is* that?"

"Boiled kelp," said my dad. "Seaweed. Supposedly it's delicious. And good for you."

FACT: Nothing good for you tastes good. Everybody knows that.

"For breakfast?" I moaned. "Yeah, no." I headed to the cabinet to grab some Super Sugar Flakies.

"Not today, Jimmy," said my dad. "It's time to try something new."

Wait a second. I'd been eating Super Sugar Flakies ever since I found out that Jonah Forrester ate them to help convince people he wasn't a vampire. It was my morning routine!

"Dad, I eat Super Sugar Flakies every day," I complained. "So do you!"

"Well, today we're changing things up."

"This stinks." Luckily, there were some muffins on the table, so I grabbed one and took a bite. Which I immediately almost threw up.

"*Yuck!* What's in that?"

"Garlic," said my dad. "Which is also very healthy."

"I don't see a muffin on your plate."

"Already had one," he said, but I totally didn't believe him. "Now dig in."

"Fine." As I tried to force it down, there was a noise behind me. I looked down and saw Abby, sleepily wagging her tail. She took one step into the kitchen, saw me eating the garlic muffin, and immediately ran to the other end of the house.

"It's never a good sign when a dog runs away from food," I said. "Just saying."

My dad sighed. "No Super Sugar Flakies today, and that's final."

As we sat there in silence and tried to eat breakfast, I realized it was stupid arguments like this that probably made him all excited about going back to work.

9:46 A.M.

IT TOOK ME ABOUT AN HOUR TO RECOVER FROM BREAKFAST.

I think I brushed my teeth for twenty minutes, but I still couldn't get the taste out of my mouth.

FACT: Toothpaste is no match for garlic and kelp.

Finally, I was ready to get on with my day. Irwin came over, and as usual, I made him watch *STOP! POLICE!* with me. It was the episode where Hank Barlow goes undercover as a race car driver to break up an international gold-smuggling gang. He gets in a terrible accident and almost dies! But that's what I love about Hank. He has no fear—he'll do whatever it takes to fight crime.

At the end of the episode, I stood up as Hank saluted his captain.

"Catching the bad guys isn't just my job," I said, along with Hank. "It's my life."

Irwin stared at me. "You're a wacko, you know that?"

"Takes one to know one," I said back. Not exactly original, I know, but it was all I could think of at the time.

We were about to start a second episode when my dad hollered, "THAT'S ENOUGH TELEVISION! GO OUTSIDE, NOW!"

"He's nervous about his job interview," I explained to Irwin. "That's why he's yelling."

"My mom does the same exact thing when I'm inside on a nice day," he answered. "But she yells even louder." That's Irwin for you. He always has to top you at everything, even if it was about how mean parents could be.

We went outside and spent five minutes blinking up into the bright sunlight, trying to figure out what to do.

"Let's go to the Boathouse," Irwin suggested.

"Good idea."

The Boathouse was an old abandoned beach club about a mile away, next to Nash's Swamp. (It used to be called Nash's Pond, but over time it kind of dried up and turned into a swamp.) No one ever went there anymore, so Irwin and I always had the place to ourselves.

"Dad, we're going to Nash's Swap!" I yelled. "We'll be back in like an hour! I'm taking Abby!"

"Are you sure you can handle it?" he yelled back.

"Yup!"

"Okay, great!"

Nothing makes parents more trusting of their kids than the prospect of getting them out of the house for a while.

We went to find Abby, who'd gone back to sleep upstairs in my closet. She looked up at us with groggy eyes, then finally agreed to get up—I think just to make me happy.

Outside, Abby took one look at the sunlight and ran straight toward the crawlspace beneath the house.

"Not today, Ab," I said. "We're taking a walk."

As I dragged her out from under the house, I remembered the guy at the rescue center, who told me that she had some kind of eye condition that made her sensitive to light. But then I thought about all her other interesting qualities that made her unlike any other dog I'd ever seen. Like how tired she seemed during the day. And how awake she seemed at night. And how she saw the garlic muffins and ran the other way. And the size of her fangs.

Especially the size of her fangs.

10:34 A.M.

AT THE BOATHOUSE, IRWIN AND I DID WHAT WE ALWAYS DO.

Argued.

Usually, we argued about sports (I liked baseball; Irwin liked football), or girls (which ones in our grade made us the most nervous, and why), or who was better at StarFighters (our favorite video game); but this time, I brought up a new topic.

"There's something different about Abby," I told Irwin, as I tied her to a tree in the shade so we could use the two tire swings.

"What do you mean?"

"I'm not sure. She kind of reminds me of Jonah Forrester."

Irwin looked at Abby, who had already fallen asleep, then rolled his eyes. "*Everything* reminds you of Jonah Forrester."

"No, I'm serious," I said. "For instance, she hates the light and sleeps all day."

He looked at me. "What's your point?"

"My point is that I think she might be more than just a typical dog."

"Like how?"

"I don't know yet." I hesitated, then decided to go for it. "I think she might be a vampire."

Irwin guffawed. "You're being completely ridiculous."

"*You're* being completely ridiculous," I answered.

"That makes no sense."

"*You* make no sense."

"Cut it out!"

"*You* cut it out!"

Hey, I never said eleven-year-old boys were the greatest arguers in the world.

After swinging got boring, we headed up to the roof-deck, where there was a broken old hot tub and beach chairs and stuff.

"Last one up is a rotten egg!" I hollered, racing up the stairs.

"Cheater!" he yelled back. "You got a head start!"

After I got up to the roof, I started doing a victory dance. "So what? I win!"

Suddenly, Irwin shouted, "Look out!"

I looked down. *Yikes!* There was this rotted plank of wood on the roof that you had to avoid, next to the hot tub—and I'd almost stepped right on it.

"Jeez," I said. "Thanks."

FACT: Friends are good to argue with, but they're even better to make sure you don't go crashing through the floor.

"You're welcome," Irwin said.

I took a deep breath and looked around. The roof was cool because it made you feel like you were on top of the world—if the world was a dried-up old swamp with two rusted-out canoes tied to a broken dock.

Irwin walked right to the edge of the roof and yelled, "HELLO OUT THERE! IT'S ME, KING OF THE WORLD!" like he always did.

I stayed far away from the edge, because I was totally scared of heights, and yelled, "SOME THINGS ARE WORTH FIGHTING FOR . . . BUT JUSTICE IS WORTH BITING FOR!" like I always did.

"Stop quoting Hank Barlow," Irwin said.

"Duh, that's Jonah Forrester," I corrected him. "*Biting*?"

"Who cares," Irwin answered.

"I do!" I said angrily, already forgetting that Irwin had basically saved my life thirty-eight seconds earlier.

I looked down and noticed that Abby, who'd been napping under the tree, was now wide-awake, looking up at me and jumping up and down.

"Look!" I said to Irwin. "She loves Jonah! Watch." I yelled again, "SOME THINGS ARE WORTH FIGHTING FOR . . . BUT JUSTICE IS WORTH BITING FOR!" And

Abby started barking like crazy and jumping higher and higher. Her jumps were practically halfway up the tree!

"So what?" Irwin said. "Now you're going to tell me she understands English? Maybe she just has to go to the bathroom."

After a minute, Abby stopped jumping and let out about a two-minute yawn.

I smacked Irwin on the shoulder. "Come on, you gotta admit, she's amazing," I said. "No dog jumps that high. And no dog yawns for that long. That was a total vampire yawn."

"You know something?" Irwin responded. "I consider myself a pretty good friend. I watch *STOP! POLICE!* with you, and I let you tell me all about your Jonah Forrester books. But I don't really want to listen to you talk about how Abby is some kind of Dracula dog. So do you mind not talking about it anymore?"

"That's fair."

"Thank you."

We were quiet for five seconds.

"You gotta admit though, that was a pretty long yawn," I said.

11:18 A.M.

ON THE WAY HOME, ABBY GNAWED ON HER LEASH.

"See?" I said to Irwin, unable to help myself. "She chews on everything."

"The teacher assignments are supposed to come today." Irwin said, completely ignoring me.

"Who cares," I answered, trying to ignore him back.

I didn't want to talk about school, because it just reminded me of my blotch and made me nervous—but Irwin was right, it was all about which teacher you got. I was hoping for Mrs. Sweetnam, who kept a jar of jelly beans on her desk at all times. And I was praying I wouldn't get Mr. Brinkmeyer, whose breath smelled like burning tires.

I was trying to figure out a way to change the subject, when we turned the corner and saw a bunch of kids playing kickball in the park. The first kid I recognized gave me a weird, nervous feeling in my stomach.

Baxter Bratford.

PROFILE

Name: Baxter Bratford

Age: 11, but looks 14

Occupation: Bully

Interests: Picking on people not his own size

Ugh.

Baxter Bratford was the biggest kid in our grade. He was also the loudest and most obnoxious. And he was definitely the baldest. Some kids said he was bald because he pulled all his hair out in a childhood tantrum, others said it was because of some weird thing that ran in his family—either way, it made him self-conscious, and angry, and eventually, just mean. But the worst thing about Baxter was that he'd had it in for me ever since first grade, when I tattled on him for sticking gum between the pages of his music book. (That was really dumb of me, looking back on it.) My parents called him a "garden-variety bully," which doesn't seem to make any sense, since I thought gardens were supposed to be pretty and nice.

Baxter was wearing his favorite outfit—baggy shorts and a blue-and-white-striped shirt that read BARNABY BRATFORD'S BESTEST BABYSITTERS on the back. Yup—Baxter's father owned the company that sent us Mrs. Cragg. So even his *dad* had it in for me.

"Keep walking," I said to Irwin.

"Not so fast!" he said, pointing. "Look."

I looked. There she was.

Daisy Flowers.

PROFILE

Name: Daisy Flowers

I know I already profiled her, but it's nice to have an excuse to talk about her again. I apologize for this short delay.

Oh no! Daisy was playing kickball with Baxter Bratford!

Double ugh.

I felt incredibly jealous that I didn't even have the nerve to talk to Daisy but somehow Baxter had gotten her to play kickball with him and his friends.

"I don't care," I said. "I'm still not stopping."

Irwin started jumping up and down. "Come on! This is our chance! You can tell her about your dog that might have special powers!"

I didn't know what to do. I definitely didn't want to deal with Baxter. But I didn't want Irwin to know I was scared of him either. And maybe I *could* tell Daisy about Abby. I had a feeling she was a dog person.

I was trying to make up my mind when Baxter made it up for me.

"Well, lookee here!" he crowed, noticing us. "If it isn't Swimmy Jimmy!"

Baxter had called me Swimmy Jimmy ever since I failed my safety test at the Y three years earlier. It wasn't even swimming, it was treading water!

I hated that nickname.

At that point, we had no choice but to walk over. A

bunch of other kids were there too. They all waved when they saw us coming. We waved back.

"Hey, Swimmy," Baxter said. "What are you doing outside? Shouldn't you be in your dorkcave reading like your fifty thousandth vampire book?" Then he guffawed at his own unfunny joke.

Abby growled. Baxter looked down at her and laughed.

"That's one ugly dog you got there, by the way," he sneered.

"I think he's cute," said Daisy, which clinched it—she was truly, actually, perfect.

"He's a she," I said dumbly.

"Who cares?" Baxter muttered. Then he turned his attention back to the game. He was pitching, of course. But instead of rolling the ball like a regular person, he was bouncing it in, which made it almost impossible to kick.

"Strike three!" Baxter screamed as some poor kid swung his leg and missed.

"Maybe you should let somebody else pitch," Daisy suggested.

Baxter glared at her. "Mind your own business." Then,

glancing over at Irwin, he added, "Get out here, we need a right fielder."

Irwin looked both horrified and flattered, since he'd never been asked to join a game in his life. "Me?"

Baxter nodded, with a look of disgust. "Do you see another dweebazoid here? Yeah, you."

Irwin ran out there as if right field were the best position in the world, as opposed to the worst position in the world, which it actually was.

I closed my eyes and said a short prayer, then walked up to Daisy.

"You really think my dog is cute?" I asked.

"I totally do!" Daisy said, kneeling down to pet Abby. Then she looked up at me and frowned. "Oh my gosh, what happened to your face?"

Uh-oh. *My blotch!*

For a minute there, I'd forgotten all about it. My heart started pounding.

"Uh . . . I gotta go," I said, grabbing Abby's leash and turning to run back to my house. I took about three steps before a big meaty paw stopped me.

"Where ya goin'?" Baxter growled.

I looked up at him. It was a pretty long ways up, since

he was about five inches taller than me.

"Um, just home."

Baxter stared down at me. "You leave when I say you can leave." Then he grinned. "Besides, you're not going anywhere until you tell us what that thing on your face is." He turned around to the rest of the kids. "Hey, guys! Come see what happened to Swimmy! It's awesome!"

FACT: Bully + Blotch = Bad Combination

Everyone came over to take a look. It seemed like none of them really wanted to be mean about it, but as soon as Baxter started laughing, they all laughed too. That's how these things work: if a bully starts making fun of some kid, you make fun of them too—because if you *don't*, chances are you might be next.

The only two kids who weren't laughing were Irwin and Daisy.

"Stop it," I begged Baxter.

Baxter shrugged. "Stop what? All I'm doing is trying to look at your face without gagging." He turned to Daisy. "Take a look!"

Daisy stood there frozen for a second. "I have to go," she said. Then she turned around and ran down the street toward her house. Since she was pretty new in town, she probably didn't want to get involved.

I can't say I blamed her.

Irwin went running after Daisy. "Where are you going?" he called to her. "Don't go!" But she never looked back, and after a minute, he turned around and came back.

"Awwwwwww." Baxter snickered. "Isn't this just so sweet and precious. Wonk is in love with Daisy Flowers!"

"I am not," Irwin insisted, as all the kids shifted their attention from my face to Irwin's lack-of-love life.

I suddenly felt incredibly relieved that no one was looking at me and my blotch anymore—which explains why I said what I said next.

"You are kind of in love with her, Irwin," I blurted out. "It's totally obvious."

Irwin's mouth dropped open, and he stared at me with a hurt look in his eyes. I immediately felt as guilty as I'd ever felt in my life.

"I didn't mean it like that," I mumbled, but it was too late.

"Forget you guys!" Irwin yelled, and he took off down the street before anyone could see him start to cry.

"Later, Wonkmeister!" Baxter crowed. Then he looked back at me, and I was sure he was going to torture me some more, but for some reason he decided not to.

"Let's play ball!" he announced. Then he looked at me. "Scarface, you in?"

Scarface? Suddenly, "Swimmy" didn't seem so bad.

I tried to stare at him without fear. "No."

"Why not?" Baxter said, walking toward me. "Your little nerd buddy just left, and now we need a right fielder."

"I just don't feel like it."

Baxter kept coming. "Well, what if I don't care *what* you feel like?"

I wasn't sure what to do. Baxter was practically two inches from my face. I was about to make a run for it when I heard something below me.

A growl.

I looked down, and there was Abby, looking at Baxter like he was an oversize groundhog.

She growled again, louder.

"Tell your mutt to be quiet," Baxter said, practically growling himself.

"I can't really tell her what to do," I muttered apologetically.

Baxter took another step toward me, and Abby suddenly let out the fiercest bark I ever heard and bared her teeth. Out came the fangs.

Baxter ran about twelve steps backward in less than a second.

"That dog's crazy!" he yelped.

"I guess that's one word for it," I said.

Baxter was breathing hard. I don't think I'd ever seen him scared before. "Well, it figures you'd need your little doggy to protect you," he said. "You better get out of here before I use her for kicking practice."

Abby was still growling softly. I wanted to say something—I wanted to tell Baxter I could protect myself!—but for some reason, I just took off down the street.

Instead of going home, I ran to Irwin's house so I could apologize.

I rang the doorbell for ten minutes.

He never answered.

11:38 A.M.–6:32 P.M.

HERE'S HOW THE REST OF THE DAY WENT:

I stared at my blotch in the mirror.

I thought about Daisy.

I felt bad about Irwin.

I tried to scrub my blotch off with soap, but it didn't work.

I tried to scrub my blotch off with a toothbrush, which made it worse.

I thought about Daisy.

I tried to call Irwin.

I answered the door to let Mrs. Cragg in.

I wished my dad luck when he left for his job interview.

I took Abby outside, and she immediately ran under the house again. When I asked my sister to help me get her out, she rolled her eyes at me and said, "I have to pick out my clothes for tomorrow."

I stared at my blotch some more.

I read fifty pages of *Fang Goodness.*

I watched two episodes of *STOP! POLICE!*

I smelled a new gross smell coming from the kitchen.

Oh, and I thought about Daisy.

6:33 P.M.

"DINNER!"

I was still outside trying to get Abby out from under the house when Mrs. Cragg screamed. Her voice sounded like a baboon beating up a violin. I'd already decided there was no way I was going anywhere near that kitchen. No way, no how.

Until Mrs. Cragg marched outside and folded her arms.

FACT: When an old-lady babysitter folds her arms, you do what she says.

"Do I want to know what's for dinner?" I asked.

Mrs. Cragg laughed. "It's good for you, that's all you need to know."

Suddenly, I heard a noise and looked down. Abby! She'd finally come out from under the house, to see what was going on. Either that, or because the sun was finally behind the trees.

Mrs. Cragg wrinkled her nose. "I want that dog outside while you have dinner."

"No," I said, surprising myself. "She's my dog, and I want her with me."

Mrs. Cragg looked like she was about to argue, but then Abby let out a low growl, so instead she just turned and walked inside.

When I got to the kitchen, my nostrils actually literally shriveled up and died. Okay, not actually literally. But the dinner stink was even more powerful than the breakfast stink. I'm glad I can't tell you what it smelled like, because that would mean I'd smelled something like it before, and luckily I hadn't. But there's a first time for everything, I guess.

Misty stuck her head in. "I'm not staying for dinner, but thanks anyway," she announced.

"Wait a second—did you clear this with your parents?" asked Mrs. Cragg, but Misty just waved and walked away.

I stared jealously at my fourteen-year-old sister. *Wow,* I thought, *what a difference three years make.*

Mrs. Cragg put a plate down in front of me. I looked at the contents—some sort of mushy red blob smothered in green gloop.

I blinked at Mrs. Cragg. "Are you serious?"

"Very," she said. Her slightly evil smile reminded me of Johnny Casper, the vampire hunter in the Jonah Forrester books. Johnny would sing and whistle every time he tried to kill Jonah. He acted like he was being all nice and helping mankind and stuff, but secretly he was evil. I hated Johnny Casper.

"I'd rather not," I moaned. "I'll just go straight to dessert, if that's all right."

"Would it be all right with your parents if you just ate sugar for the rest of your life?" asked Mrs. Cragg. "Would it be all right with your parents if all of your teeth fell out?"

Was she actually talking to me about *teeth*?

I was about to argue, but when I saw her own yellow choppers shining down on me, I shut my mouth and sat at the table.

FACT: Looking at someone's yellow teeth does not increase your appetite.

"What *is* this stuff anyway?" I asked, even though I was pretty sure I didn't want to know the answer.

"Fried beets in pea sauce," answered Mrs. Cragg. "Eat it and you'll live to be a hundred years old."

"I don't want to be a hundred if I have to eat this stuff. I don't even want to live until *tomorrow* if I have to eat this stuff."

Mrs. Cragg laughed, but not in an I-think-you're-funny way.

I felt a brush against my leg. I looked down and saw Abby peering up at me. She was trying to tell me something, but I wasn't sure what. Then I saw her eyes, moving back and forth from me to my plate. That was it! She was willing to eat this gross food for me! What an amazing dog!

I waited until Mrs. Cragg started washing a pot in the sink, then I quickly shoveled the food down to Abby. She scarfed every bite in about three seconds. Unbelievably, she seemed to like it. This was going to work out great! I was saved!

Until I wasn't.

The first thing that happened was I heard a gross noise. It sounded kind of like *thlarpksh!*

FACT: When you hear the noise *thlarpksh!*, you know it's not good.

Yup. You guessed it.

Abby vomited up pretty much everything I'd just given her. I guess fried beets aren't the best thing for a dog's diet after all.

Mrs. Cragg whipped her head around. "What was that?" Then her eyes darted to the floor, where Abby was standing right next to a reddish-greenish-globbish-gloopish pile of *gross*.

Abby started wagging her tail. Believe it or not, I think she wanted more.

She wasn't going to get it.

Especially since she jumped up on the counter and threw up a tiny bit more—and some got on Mrs. Cragg's beloved, perfectly combed red hair.

She screamed, "MY HAIR!!!!" and then made a sickening noise that sounded kind of like *AARHROO-ARAHHHREEK!*

FACT: *AARHROOARAHHHREEK!* is even worse than *thlarpksh!*

Mrs. Cragg hooked my arm with her cane and screamed, "What did you do? Did you give that dog your dinner? DID YOU?"

"Sh-she was hungry," I stammered.

"That's it!" Mrs. Cragg howled. "I've had it with you and this dog! You both need to learn a lesson!" Then she grabbed Abby by the collar. I couldn't tell which one of them was barking and growling louder.

I ran after them as they rounded the corner and headed straight for the hall closet. "Wait!" I shouted, but I was too late—Mrs. Cragg opened the closet and threw Abby in. Then she slammed the door shut.

"It's nice and dark in there, just the way you like it!" she yelled through the door.

"She likes *my* closet, not the hall closet!" I said, with tears in my eyes.

"Well, I'm a babysitter, not a dogsitter," she muttered. "She stays in there until your parents come home." Then she clomped away, her cane hitting the floor with an angry *smack!*

Soon she was going to be a no-sitter, if I had anything to say about it.

7:12 P.M.

I SAT NEXT TO THE CLOSET, THINKING, trying to figure out what to do next. But it was hard to concentrate, because of all the noise going on in the kitchen. Pots were rattling, water was running, and Mrs. Cragg was . . . *singing*. That's right, my babysitter was having a great time, singing at the top of her lungs, while my dog was stuck in a closet that might as well have been a dungeon.

It would have been so easy to just let Abby out! But if she ran into the kitchen and did something else to make Mrs. Cragg upset, then who knows what would happen.

"Are you okay, Abby?" I whispered through the door. "Hang in there, I'll figure something out."

No response.

"Yum, yum, yum!" I heard Mrs. Cragg exclaim. I guess she was about to sit down to her own plate of fried *blech*.

"I'm going to go talk to her right now," I whispered to Abby, even though I wasn't moving.

Come on! I said to myself. *Be brave!*

I heard a slight scratch on the door. Abby was giving me courage!

After a few deep breaths, I walked into the kitchen.

Guess what I saw?

Mrs. Cragg was sitting down to dinner, all right, but there wasn't a fried beet in sight. Instead, I was staring at a cheeseburger, french fries, and chocolate milk.

FACT: Adults never actually eat the disgusting stuff they feed you.

She looked up at me impatiently. "What is it?"

"You need to let Abby out of the closet," I said. "I promise she'll be good."

"That dog doesn't know *how* to be good," said Mrs. Cragg, spraying french fry particles out of her mouth. "The answer is no."

I stood up to my full height (not very full) and took a deep breath. "This is behavior that no civilized society can accept," I said, my voice shaking a little. "And I will do everything in my power to stop it."

Mrs. Cragg's eyes went wide. "What did you just say?"

I wasn't sure I could repeat it. And I definitely didn't want to tell her that it was exactly what Hank Barlow said, whenever he was about to catch the bad guy.

Be like Hank, I said to myself. *You can do it.*

"I said, this is behavior—"

"I HEARD YOU!" she yelled. "Now leave me alone. Scram."

But I refused to scram. I might not have been the bravest guy in the world, but I refused to be a coward.

I was trying to figure out what to do next, when I saw something that made me rub my eyes.

The closet door handle was *moving*.

I rubbed my eyes again.

Still moving.

Then, unbelievably, I saw the door start to open.

Are you kidding me?!?

Meanwhile, Mrs. Cragg crammed another bite of burger in her mouth and closed her eyes in delight. She had no idea what Abby was doing.

"Uh . . . okay," I said to Mrs. Cragg. "I guess you're right. I guess we'll wait until my parents get home." My plan was to wait until Abby had somehow miraculously finished opening the door—then I'd yell, "Holy smokes! Abby got out!" And while Mrs. Cragg freaked out, I'd grab Abby and hide her in my room.

But that turned out to not be Abby's plan.

Because two seconds later, the door opened all the way and I suddenly saw two eyes looking at me like glow-in-the-dark marbles.

I tried to whisper to Abby to not move, but it didn't work.

Instead, she sprinted straight for us. I think she wanted to see if there were any leftover fried beets.

"WAIT!" I yelled, but it was too late.

Mrs. Cragg looked up in shock. "What the—?" But she

never got to finish the sentence, because Abby crashed into her, knocked the cheeseburger out of her hands, and ate it, all in about four seconds.

Mrs. Cragg's face turned the color of the beets she'd tried to get me to eat. Meanwhile, Abby started in on the fries.

Then I saw something I'd never seen before, and hope to never see again.

I saw a human being actually try to smack an animal.

Notice I said *try*.

Mrs. Cragg swatted at Abby's adorable little nose, but Abby was way too fast for the old lady and ducked out of the way.

Which is when the fangs came out.

"Abby, no!" I yelled—as if that would do any good. She was in full predator mode. She started growling and walking slowly toward Mrs. Cragg, whose face went from beet red to pea green.

"Get that beast away from me!" she yelled, backing up and bumping into the table. Plates and glasses crashed to the floor, but Abby didn't care. She crouched down, like you see on one of those nature shows, where the panther suddenly spots the defenseless gazelle.

In case you were wondering, Mrs. Cragg was the gazelle.

Then Abby jumped, right onto Mrs. Cragg's shoulder.

"Abby, no!" I said again, even though what I was thinking was, *Reminds me of Jonah Forrester.*

Mrs. Cragg let out a bloodcurdling scream— "AARRHHHGGGHHH!!!"—just as the front door opened. I turned to look—it was my mom, who picked that second to *finally* come home from work. She heard Mrs. Cragg scream, sprinted past me into the kitchen, and pulled Abby away, just as she was about to sink her teeth in.

"What on earth is going on here?" my mom yelled.

I wasn't sure what to say. I ended up going with "Not much," which probably wasn't the best choice.

Mrs. Cragg grabbed my mom's arm. "Mrs. Bishop," she panted, "this dog tried to kill me. Well, first she acted crazy, and then she threw up all over the kitchen, and then she was just about to bite me! I'm sure if you hadn't walked in when you did, I would be terribly injured right now. Or worse!"

I couldn't believe my ears. "That's not the whole story!" I protested. "This crazy old lady tried to feed me gross fried beets, and she ordered me to eat the whole thing, and so I gave it to Abby, and yeah, Abby vomited it all up, but then Mrs. Cragg locked her in the closet! And after that she tried to punch Abby! She's a horrible babysitter, Mom, I swear!"

Abby, who was still in my mom's arms, squirmed in agreement.

My mom shook her head. "Jimmy, I saw what I saw with my own eyes. Abby wasn't locked in the closet, she was right here, attacking poor Mrs. Cragg."

"That's because somehow she broke out! Abby broke out of the closet! I swear: it was just like on *STOP! POLICE!* when Hank Barlow broke out of that car trunk during the episode where he was being held hostage by the gang of hippies!" I stopped talking when I realized my mom was staring at me like I was a crazy person.

"Honey, this isn't a television show from fifty years ago," my mom said slowly, like I was a toddler. "This is real life." Finally, she took her eyes off me and looked at Mrs. Cragg. "I'm so, so sorry," she said. "I will deal with this."

"I certainly hope so," Mrs. Cragg said.

My mom waited a few seconds for everyone to calm

down, then asked Mrs. Cragg, "Can you still come tomor-row after school? Again, I'm so sorry."

The babysitter smiled sweetly. "I accept your apology," she said, nodding. "And yes, I will come tomorrow. But if things don't improve, it will have to be my last day. I'm sure you understand. Good night." Then she turned to me, nodded, and walked out the door.

"Mom!" I said, but she refused to look at me. Instead, she looked at the broken plates on the table, beet stains on the wall, and dog vomit on the floor.

"We'll discuss this with Dad when he gets home," she said.

"Discuss what?" I moaned.

"Everything," said my mom. "Including the possibil-ity that keeping Abby might not be such a great idea right now."

"No way!" I screamed. "That's not fair! You don't know what happened! You're never here! And Dad is here but trying not to be! You guys don't care about Misty or Abby or me at all!"

"That's ridiculous, Jimmy, you know we love you," said my mom, but I was already halfway up the stairs, and I pretended I didn't even hear her.

9:33 P.M.

FOR THE NEXT HOUR OR SO I HUNG OUT WITH ABBY IN MY ROOM, reading *Fang Goodness*. I was just getting to the best part—where someone is robbing movie sets, so Jonah Forrester goes undercover as an actor to play a vampire in a movie, but the director doesn't know he's a real vampire, he just thinks Jonah is a really good actor—when my dad got home.

He poked his head in to tell me his interview went really well, and asked if I wanted to talk about the dog situation. I told him congratulations but that I didn't feel much like talking. I just wanted to be alone with my dog.

"You told mom that Abby let herself out of the closet?" Dad asked.

I nodded. "She totally did, Dad. I swear!"

"Okay, honey," said my dad. "Okay." He paused for a second. "You know that door has a loose handle, right? It opens on its own all the time."

"I know," I said. "But it's not what happened this time. I promise, I'm not lying!"

He started to leave, then turned back. "By the way, the medicine for your rash won't be in until tomorrow. Mom will pick it up after work."

"Great," I said. "Just in time for me to already have been humiliated at school."

"Now, come on," said my dad. "You'll be fine in no time."

"I'm not giving Abby up."

My dad sighed. "Well, we'll see, but your mom's not happy right now. I have one last interview tomorrow, to meet the big boss. We're going to give it one more try with Mrs. Cragg. That dog needs to win her over, and fast."

I couldn't believe it. "So you'd rather keep Mrs. Cragg than Abby?"

My dad sighed. "I'd rather keep you both. So figure it out." He kissed the top of my head. "Don't forget to walk the dog before bed."

After he left, I hugged Abby. "We're sticking together," I told her. "You're special. You're different. We'll figure some-thing out. You just need to not vomit on the babysitter anymore." Abby gave me a quick lick on the hand, but mainly she was looking out the window. It was nighttime, so of course she was back on high alert.

I thought of the night before, when I was pretty sure she'd snuck out the window while I was sleeping.

"What are you up to?" I whispered. "What kind of a dog are you?" But she didn't answer.

By the time I took Abby for her walk it was dark out, so I got my flashlight. As soon as I opened the back door Abby pulled on the leash so hard, I had to run to keep up.

She started sniffing around the yard, like she was looking for a rematch with the groundhog.

"Not tonight, Abby," I begged.

Her next stop was a bush next to the barbecue grill, where she started gnawing on something, probably an old bone.

"Hey, Ab, whatcha got there?" I said, but she kept on chomping. I was trying to figure out how to get Abby back in the house, when she suddenly froze, stopped chewing, and looked up.

"What is it, girl?" I asked, but she still didn't move. So I froze too. Then I heard it.

It sounded like talking.

We both stood there for another second, listening.

It stopped, then the talking started again, a little louder, like arguing.

FACT: If there was a list of things that you'd be happy to hear, two strange voices outside your house late at night would be pretty much at the bottom of that list.

"Who could that be?" I whispered.

I was just about to go inside and get my parents, when Abby suddenly gave a short growl and took off, yanking the leash right out of my hand. I stood there frozen for another second, then sprinted after her as she darted around to the front of the house.

Two people were standing right in front of our house. It was too dark to really see what they looked like—all I could see was that one was wearing a striped shirt.

They were yelling at each other.

"You were supposed to bring it to me tonight!" the first one said.

"It's too dangerous!" the second one said.

"Then tomorrow . . . or else!" the first one said.

What in the world?

My skin grew cold with fear. I'd seen enough episodes

of *STOP! POLICE!* to know that two strangers fighting right outside your house late at night were probably up to no good.

Abby wasn't scared at all though. In fact, she was the opposite of scared. She sprinted out to the street, started barking at the top of her lungs, and then flashed her extremely large fangs.

The two people took one look at her and started running.

I was too nervous to move, but Abby sure wasn't. She started chasing them and was nipping at their heels by the time they reached their car, climbed in, and took off down the street. Abby kept chasing, barking like crazy, until she got bored—then she turned around and trotted back to me, her tail wagging like she was having the best time in the world.

It was at that point that somebody across the street in Daisy's house turned on an outside light.

Uh-oh.

The last thing I needed was for my parents to think that Abby had woken up the whole neighborhood.

I glanced back at my house. No movement. Good thing my parents liked to watch TV in their bedroom at the back of the house.

"Abby girl," I said. "We better go back inside." She wasn't listening though. She'd found something on the street that she was happily licking. I bent down to see what it was. It looked dark and sticky, and for a quick, gross second, I thought it was blood—*because vampires drink blood, remember?* But then when I looked more closely, I realized it was just a bit of melted chocolate stuck to a candy wrapper.

"Hey, someone told me that chocolate is bad for dogs," I said, taking the wrapper from Abby. Then I turned and looked down the street. "Litterers," I muttered, even though they were long gone.

Abby looked at me, like she was ready for me to tell her what our next fun activity was going to be.

"You're an amazing dog," I whispered. "But if I'm going to have any hope of keeping you at all, we need to go to bed *right now.*"

Her tail stopped wagging, which was the international dog sign for *This does not make me happy.*

"Thanks for chasing those guys away, by the way," I added. "Let's go inside."

She gave me one wag, then ran to the front door.

Yup, you heard me.

She *listened.*

10:12 P.M.

ONCE WE WERE BACK INSIDE, safe and sound, Abby settled at her spot, staring out the window. First I made sure the window was totally shut, then I laid down on the bed, thinking about all her unusual habits:

She sleeps all day.

She's up all night.

She hates the light.

She's got huge fangs, and she's not afraid to use them.

She scared off two bad people who were arguing in front of our house.

Wait a second.

I picked up my copy of *Fang Goodness* and flipped through the pages until I found what I was looking for.

Of all the things that were most frustrating for Jonah, he felt that having a secret identity was the hardest of all. No one could know who he really was; that would ruin everything. So he had to be satisfied living two very separate existences: the life of an ordinary, everyday man, going about his business . . . and the life he led after dark, when his true self emerged and his true soul was revealed.

So *that was it.*

I closed the book.

I didn't care if anyone believed me, I knew the truth.

It was official.

Abby wasn't just a vampire dog.

She was a crime-fighting vampire dog.

PART THREE

THE BAD, BAD BABYSITTER

THURSDAY, AUGUST 28

7:09 A.M.

I WOKE UP AND IMMEDIATELY THOUGHT, *First day of school.*

Then I thought, *Oh, jeez, the babysitter comes back today with more horrible recipes.*

Then I thought, *Better keep Abby away from Mrs. Cragg. Because if she tries to bite her again, my parents will make me give her back. Which would be horrible, because I love her, and I'd miss her, and because she's a crime-fighting vampire dog.*

And then I tiptoed past Abby (who of course was now fast asleep), headed to the bathroom, and looked in the mirror.

Which made me think, *BLOTCH!!!*

It was *huge* again.

California?

Bigger.

Texas??

Bigger.

Alaska???

Bingo.

It was official. My blotch had made it all the way up to the very largest state in the country. The tip of the blotch started at my left eyebrow, wound its way down past my ear, took a right near my jaw, and ended by my right cheek. It was redder than ever too.

And did I mention that it was a little scaly, kind of like an iguana? I don't think they have iguanas in Alaska, but whatever. You get my point.

Misty poked her head in and screamed, "I need the bathroom!" It was her first day of school too—her first day of high school, in fact—and she looked just as nervous as me. Then she saw my blotch, and I thought she was about to say "EEEWW!" just like last time, but she didn't. She just said, "Jeez. Take your time."

FACT: When your incredibly annoying and self-centered older sister actually feels sorry for you, you know you've got a real problem.

Then she added, "Hey, you better make sure Abby's a good girl today."

I nodded. "I will. This whole thing is all Mrs. Cragg's fault. She's crazy! She locked Abby in the closet! But Abby's amazing, she broke out herself! And I didn't tell Mom and Dad, but during our walk before bed, Abby chased away two people who were staking out our house! I think they were bad guys—that maybe they were going to rob us!"

"Oooookay," Misty said, in that way that means, *I think you might need to see a doctor.*

"I know you don't believe me, but it's true! Abby—" I stopped.

Misty looked at me. "Abby what?"

"Nothing." I realized I shouldn't talk about Abby being a crime-fighting vampire dog. It would just make people think I was a total crazy person. Even more than they already do.

"Well, if you just train the dog, she'll be fine," Misty said. "I don't want to give her back either. She is kind of cute."

"She doesn't need any training," I said. "And she's way more than cute." I started furiously rubbing my blotch with a washcloth.

Misty shook her head sadly. "Um, it's not like it's a

stain, you know. I don't think it's gonna come out. And no offense or anything, but could you stand like really far away from me at the bus stop?"

"Sure." I sighed, stopped scrubbing, went back to my room, and scooped Abby up in my arms. She was sleepy, of course, since it was daytime. I headed downstairs for breakfast. My parents were sitting at the table.

"Mom!" I said. "What are you still doing here?"

She got up and hugged me. "Are you kidding? It's the first day of school! You better believe I'm going to see my babies off." Then she took a look at my blotch. "Not so bad," she said, completely lying. "When I get home tonight, that thing is going *down!*"

"What time is Mrs. Cragg getting here today?" I said, changing the subject.

"She'll be here when you get home from school," my mom said. "Which reminds me, Dad had a good idea."

He nodded. "It might be nice for the two of you to have some time together without any Abby distractions, so I thought maybe she'd take you to the park after school, while your sister watches Abby. Does that sound fun?"

I felt my blotch start to get hot. "Actually, no," I said. "I'd rather hang out with Abby than Mrs. Cragg. She hates dogs. And she hates Abby most of all. She will figure out a way for you guys to hate her too."

My parents looked at each other. "Honey, it's a stressful time right now," my mom said, "with school starting, and your rash—"

"The only thing that's stressful is that babysitter!" I interrupted.

"Jimmy, you're a smart kid," said my dad, a little more firmly. "We can't have a dog that bites people. You know that."

I suddenly realized I couldn't win the argument and I was tired of trying. "Fine. I don't care anymore."

Then I ran out the front door, ran right past Misty, right past Mom and Dad, and right past our bus stop. I didn't stop until I got to school, which was a mile and a half away.

(OTHERWISE KNOWN AS THE LONGEST MORNING OF MY LIFE)

FACT: If you want to feel popular, visit an animal shelter. If you want to feel the opposite of popular, show up for the first day of school with a blotch on your face.

When I got to school, the other kids didn't really know how to deal with my blotch.

Some looked grossed out. Some laughed. Some looked away. Some took pictures with their cell phones. Some were nice about it and tried to smile.

One kid just stared at me for about a minute, then said, "At least it's not cancer."

Which made me wonder: *What if it is cancer?*

123

The teachers all tried to ignore it, but they weren't really successful.

And Irwin was still mad at me for telling everyone at the kickball game he was in love with Daisy, so he was absolutely no help.

The first three hours of school felt like a year.

Then, finally, it was recess. But instead of going to the playground like all the other kids, I got my copy of *Fang Goodness* out of my backpack and headed to the library. I opened it up to one of my favorite chapters.

There were times when Jonah wondered if he'd be alone forever. Who would marry one of his kind? What mere mortal would take on the epic challenge of loving one such as he?

He took to wandering the streets at night, peering into the windows of restaurants and bars and watching people laugh, and talk, and touch. He longed for such a connection but was convinced it would never come.

And then, in an instant, everything changed.

Jonah saw her.

Olivia.

She was waiting to cross the street, looking at
her watch, when she—

"What are you doing?"

I blinked my eyes and looked up. Irwin was standing over me with his arms crossed.

"Huh?"

"What are you doing?" he asked again. "Can't you ever stop reading that book?"

"I'm just getting to the good part."

Irwin shrugged. "Whatever," he said, and started walking away.

I watched him go, then suddenly jumped to my feet. "Wait!"

He waited for me to catch up.

"Hey, Irwin, I . . . about the game yesterday—"

"I don't want to talk about it."

"It's just that . . . I was feeling really embarrassed about my blotch and I guess I was happy that you were being made fun of too. It was really dumb."

"Okay," Irwin said, looking at the floor.

I wasn't done. "But also, it would be good if you stopped making fun of me all the time for liking Jonah

Forrester and *STOP! POLICE!* When you do that it kind of makes me feel like a loser."

"I don't make fun of you!" Irwin protested.

"You just did!"

"Well, if I do, it's just because sometimes it seems like you like that stuff more than me."

I was surprised. "What are you talking about?"

Irwin stopped walking. "I'm talking about how whenever I want to do something, you'd rather just watch some stupid cop show or read some stupid vampire book."

"That's not true," I said, even though as I said it, I was thinking, *That's true.*

"Let's just forget it," Irwin said.

"I'm sorry if you're sorry," I said.

"I'm sorry if you're sorry," Irwin said back.

Irwin turned and looked at me for the first time during the whole conversation. "Best friends are supposed to stick together so that when people make fun of one of us, the other one will be there to make him feel better."

I suddenly felt really grateful to have a friend who could say such simple but true things.

"Yeah," I said.

He smacked my back. "Let's go to the playground."

As soon as we got outside though, the happiness I felt was immediately replaced by a bad feeling in my stomach. The first thing I saw was a bunch of kids standing around the jungle gym, staring at someone at the top of the slide. They were all laughing hysterically. My heart started to pound when I looked up and saw Baxter Bratford standing there.

He'd drawn red magic marker all over his face.

"Who am I?" he yelled. "First person to guess right gets to kiss my rash!"

I felt tears start to form behind my eyes.

"We can go back inside if you want," Irwin said. But we were both frozen in place.

"Come on, who am I?!?" Baxter hollered again.

Someone raised their hand. I didn't want to know who it was, but I looked anyway.

Daisy Flowers.

She was laughing and smiling as she waved her hand in the air. "Oh, I know!" she chirped. "Pick me! I know who you are!"

I couldn't believe it. Could it be that Daisy actually liked Baxter? Even though I didn't know her very well, I never would have guessed that she would fall for someone like Baxter. Especially since it seemed like she thought he was a jerk too, at the kickball game.

"Daisy, don't," Irwin said, but she ignored him.

"Pick me!" she begged Baxter again.

He looked down at her. "Well, lookee here," he said. "The new girl suddenly wants to be my pal."

"I get it!" Daisy told him. "I know who you are!"

"Awesome!" Baxter said, with a big satisfied smile on his face. "Why don't you come up here and tell the whole world?"

"Yay!" Daisy squealed. She clapped her hands, climbed up the slide, and stood right next to Baxter, who had a big smug smile on his face.

I wanted to run away so badly, but for some reason I didn't.

"Tell everyone who I am," Baxter said.

Daisy stuck her face one inch from Baxter's.

"You're a *bully*," she announced.

Everybody gasped.

Baxter looked like *he'd* just swallowed some fried beets. "I'm a *what*?"

"You heard me," Daisy said. Then she turned and shouted it to all the kids who were staring up at her.

"BAXTER IS A BULLY, AND HE'S MEAN, AND EVERYONE HERE KNOWS IT."

FACT: A nasty jerk is no match for a perfect girl.

People just stood there, too shocked to speak. Then, everyone started talking at once. Finally, a girl named Tanya Kelley looked up at Baxter and said, "She's right. You are kind of a bully."

"Shut up, all of you!" Baxter yelled. "I was just making a joke! I was just being funny!"

"No one's laughing, Baxter," Daisy said. "I thought maybe at the kickball game you were just in a bad mood, but now I know. You're a bully. My older sister was bullied at our last school, and it was awful, and it was one of the reasons why we moved here. I promised myself I'd never let it happen again without saying something. So I'm saying something. Stop it."

I couldn't believe it. Even though I knew it was Daisy speaking, it sounded exactly like Hank Barlow.

This is behavior that no civilized society can accept. And I will do everything in my power to stop it . . .

"You heard her, Baxter," someone else said. "Stop it." I wasn't sure who said it, until I realized . . . it was *me*.

Everyone turned and stared. But the strangest thing happened. I didn't feel embarrassed. I didn't even care that I could feel my blotch burning on my face.

I felt free.

"And you're *not* funny, Baxter," I continued. "You're the *opposite* of funny."

Daisy slid down the slide, came running up to me, and took my hand.

"Jimmy is my new best friend," she said, "and I don't care who knows it."

Irwin immediately ran over too. "Sorry, but Jimmy *is* *my* best friend."

"Then I'll be his second best friend," Daisy suggested.

"And my second best friend too," Irwin insisted.

Daisy looked back and forth between Irwin and me. I think she realized that she basically wasn't going to get one of us without the other.

"Sounds good," she said, giggling.

Meanwhile, Baxter looked around and decided this was one fight he wasn't going to win. "What a lousy bunch of losers," he grumbled as he climbed down from the slide. But you know what? No one was listening to him anymore.

As we started walking back toward the school, I turned to Daisy. "That was really brave what you did."

"No it wasn't. It was just normal."

I didn't argue with her, since we all knew I was right— it *was* brave. "Hey, can I ask you something?"

She smiled. "Sure!"

"Why are you being so nice to me? I'm not exactly Mr. Popular, not to mention I have a big gross mark on my face."

Daisy looked at me. "At the kickball game, when I saw you with your dog, you just seemed . . . really nice."

"Oh, great," Irwin said. "You had to bring up the dog."

"Quiet," I told Irwin.

"Hey, how is Abby anyway?" Daisy asked.

"Oh, she's amazing," I said. "I just hope I get to keep her."

Daisy frowned. "Huh?"

"I got in a fight with my annoying babysitter, and Abby jumped on her and almost bit her, and also Abby vomited and kind of made a huge mess in the house. She was just protecting me, but my parents didn't care. They said if she doesn't learn to behave we have to bring her back to the shelter."

"Too bad you can't take your babysitter back to the shelter," Irwin said.

Daisy laughed. "Good one, Irwin!" she said. Irwin looked like he'd just won a million dollars.

"You know what though?" I said. "There's something weird about Mrs. Cragg."

"What do you mean?" Irwin asked. "She's just another annoying babysitter who makes you eat gross healthy food. What else is new?"

"It's more than that," I said. "It's like . . . it's almost like she's keeping some kind of secret or something. Not to mention the fact that she locked Abby in the closet after the whole vomiting thing."

"Which kind of makes sense, when you think about it," Irwin said unhelpfully.

"My parents don't get it," I went on. "They're so busy running around that they're totally convinced Mrs. Cragg is awesome."

Daisy looked concerned. "Well, do you want me to come over to your house after school and help you train Abby or something?"

My turn to look like I'd won a million dollars. "That would be so amazing!"

She smiled brightly. "Great. I'll see you later." Then she ran off to her classroom.

It might have been the best four seconds of my life.

But I stopped smiling when I saw how upset Irwin looked. I sighed. "Sorry, Irwin. I guess maybe she likes me a little. You can come over too, if you want."

"You don't really want me to come over," he mumbled.

"Yes, I do!"

Irwin shook his head. "I don't need you to feel sorry for me," he said. "Like the way Daisy feels sorry for you, because of that thing on your face."

"What's that supposed to mean?"

"It means she's just being nice to you because you're *ugly*!" Irwin blurted out.

My cheeks started burning. "Take that back."

But Irwin didn't say anything. He just looked ashamed and ran off.

I touched my blotch, which was red-hot. Even though I knew Irwin was just jealous, it still felt like someone had smacked me in the face. Someone who happened to be my best friend.

I stood there, wondering how I went from feeling so great one second to so lousy the next.

Man, I thought. *Could this day get any weirder?*

If I only knew.

3:15 P.M.

AFTER SCHOOL, I WAS WAITING BY THE BUS TO MEET DAISY, when I saw Irwin on his bicycle. He always biked back and forth to school.

"Is Daisy still coming over?" he asked.

I didn't answer.

"What?" he said. "You're still mad?"

"Take back what you said about my blotch. About me being ugly."

Irwin just stood there.

I shook my head. "Forget it."

He looked like he really wanted to take it back but for some reason he couldn't. Instead, he biked away.

"Hey!" yelled a voice, and I turned around. There was Daisy, coming out of the school with two girls, Mara Lloyd and Lila Egan. They started heading over to me.

Uh-oh.

This was it. The part where Daisy realizes that there are way more popular people to be hanging around with than Swimmy Jimmy.

"Okay, well, see you later," Daisy said.

I tried to act cool. "So you're not coming over after all?" I asked.

Daisy's face scrunched up in confusion. "Of course I'm coming over, silly!" she said. She pointed at the girls. "I'm saying good-bye to them."

"Oh," I said. "I knew that."

"What are we going to do at your house?" she asked. "We're going to try and train Abby, right?"

"Yup," I said. I was just about to add *And also I thought maybe we'd watch an episode or two of* STOP! POLICE! when I pictured Irwin rolling his eyes and I decided not to. "We'll figure out some other fun stuff to do too," I said instead.

Daisy smiled. "Sounds great!"

I saw Irwin in the distance, watching us from his bike, and suddenly I felt guilty. I was about to call out to him to meet us at my house, but for some reason, I didn't.

Maybe Irwin was right.

Maybe I wanted Daisy for myself after all.

3:42 P.M.

WHEN WE GOT HOME, MRS. CRAGG WAS IN THE KITCHEN, making after-school "snacks."

"Stay away from the kitchen, if you want to live," I whispered to Daisy.

"Hello there!" Mrs. Cragg sang, just as friendly as can be. Then she spotted Daisy, and her smile faded for a split second.

Daisy smiled shyly. "I'm Daisy. I live across the street."

"Hello, young lady," Mrs. Cragg said. "It's nice to meet you." Then she looked at me. "Your parents didn't say anything about a friend coming over. Have you forgotten that we're going out?"

"No, I remember," I said. "But Daisy and I thought that instead we could stay here and train Abby to be better behaved."

"I see." Mrs. Cragg thought for a second. "Well, your

parents asked us to go to the park, so we should do that. Daisy, you're welcome to come. But I don't feel comfortable taking Abby in my car. You can play with her when you get home."

I thought about it for a second, then decided not to make a big deal out of it. I had to make this work with Mrs. Cragg.

"Fine," I said. "But let me just go say hi."

"Quickly," said Mrs. Cragg.

We ran up to my room, where Abby was sleeping in the closet.

"Oh, she's so cute!" squealed Daisy.

I leaned down. "Hey, girl." Abby woke up with a wag and licked my nose. "I'll be back in a little while."

"Shouldn't we take her out to go to the bathroom?" Daisy asked.

"Of course we should!" I said, embarrassed that I didn't think of it first.

I grabbed the leash and we headed outside. Abby blinked her eyes at the sunlight, as usual. She quickly did her business and then pulled the leash toward the spot under the house where she liked to hang out.

"Not today, Ab," I said. "I need to go out for a little while. But we'll be back soon."

"Your babysitter doesn't seem so bad," Daisy said to me, as we walked Abby back to the house. "Actually, she seems really nice."

"I know," I said. "Something's different today."

Mrs. Cragg was waiting in the car. "Hurry, children," she called. "We don't want to miss the best part of the day!"

"I'm going to sit in the back, with Daisy," I told her.

Mrs. Cragg shook her head. "Oh please," she said sweetly, "sit up here with me."

"Okay." I opened the door and sat down next to her cane.

"Oh, shoot," Daisy said. "I should go check with my mom, and make sure I can go out."

For a second I saw Mrs. Cragg's eyes go dark, but then she smiled. "Well, go ahead, my dear," she said to Daisy. "Hurry along now."

Daisy ran across the street to her house, leaving Mrs. Cragg and me in the car.

"She seems like a very sweet young lady," Mrs. Cragg said.

"She is." I paused, then said, "I'm sorry that Abby and you aren't getting along. I really hope we can fix it."

Mrs. Cragg stared straight ahead. "Well, Jimmy, thank

you for saying that. And perhaps we might have been able to, indeed."

"What do you mean, *might have*?"

"Well, I'm a little too old to be chasing a puppy around," she said. "As it turns out, I've been offered a position at a nice home with no pets." She smiled at me. "So today will be my last day as your babysitter."

"Oh," I said. I couldn't believe it. My dream was coming true. No more fried beets! So why did I feel a little weird?

Daisy came back and gave the thumbs-up.

"All set," she said, hopping in the backseat.

We were just pulling into the street when I saw Mrs. Cragg glance in the rearview mirror, and her mouth fell open wide. "What on earth?"

I turned around and saw Abby sprinting down the driveway, heading right toward us.

"Abby, no!" I said, but I was too late. She jumped through the open window and landed right on my lap.

"That dog is unbelievable!" cried Mrs. Cragg.

"I'm so sorry," Daisy said. "I guess we didn't shut the front door all the way."

"Abby can open doors by herself!" I blurted out, which made Daisy look at me funny.

Meanwhile, Abby was sitting there, happy as a clam, panting away.

"Can she come, Mrs. Cragg?" I begged. "Can she, please?"

I absolutely, positively knew that Mrs. Cragg would say no.

Until she said, "Fine."

See? I told you it was a crazy day.

3:58 P.M.

THE NEXT WEIRD THING THAT HAPPENED WAS THAT INSTEAD OF GOING TO AMBLER'S GREEN, which was the popular park downtown, we went to Nash's Swamp.

"What are we doing here?" I asked.

"It's much less crowded," answered Mrs. Cragg. "This way Abby can't attack any other dogs or people."

"That wouldn't happen," I said.

"Well, if it did, you know the dog would have to go back to the shelter, and I'm sure you wouldn't want that."

"No, he wouldn't," Daisy piped in.

Mrs. Cragg smiled at Daisy through the rearview mirror. "That's right, young lady."

We pulled into an empty, long-abandoned parking lot. The only other things in it were weeds.

I looked around. "What are we supposed to do here?"

"My, aren't we full of questions today?" Mrs. Cragg

said. "You're children, I'm sure you can figure out a way to have fun."

"Too bad we don't have a ball," Daisy said. "We could have played fetch or something."

Eventually we found a stick and started throwing it to Abby. Instead of bringing it back though, she wanted to be chased. So we started chasing her all over the park, until finally Daisy threw the stick back toward the car. Abby picked it up and ran up to Mrs. Cragg, wagging her tail. Then she dropped the stick at Mrs. Cragg's feet and waited.

"Throw it to her," I called. "You can do it!"

Slowly, Mrs. Cragg bent down, picked up the stick, and tossed it a few feet. It was kind of a pathetic throw, but Abby didn't care. She tore after it, picked it up, and threw it up in the air herself! Mrs. Cragg laughed, and it seemed like a real, honest laugh.

"She really is quite cute, I must admit." Mrs. Cragg bent down to pet Abby, and for a brief second I was almost sad that she wasn't going to be my babysitter anymore.

Then we all heard the rumble of an engine. I saw Mrs. Cragg's face change. I wasn't sure why, but it changed.

Two seconds later, a van turned into the lot.

"Who the heck is that?" Daisy wondered.

The van pulled up right next to us. On the side, it read, BRATFORD'S BESTEST BABYSITTERS! TRUST YOUR KIDS WITH THE BESTEST! BETTER THAN THE RESTEST!

Huh?!?!?

The door opened and out came a very tall, very large man. He was wearing the same blue-and-white-striped shirt that Baxter Bratford always wore. He had a beard that made him look like a pirate, and he smelled like he'd just jumped in a lake of cologne.

The man saw Mrs. Cragg, smiled, and gave her a little peck on the cheek. "Nice to see you, my dear," he said.

My dear? Were they married or something?!?

Then he walked over to me, pointed at my blotch, and said, "Well hey there, Swimmy Jimmy. You should fire your tattoo guy, that didn't come out so good."

I felt my heart speed up.

"You should talk," I said back. "You're not exactly the most handsome person I've ever seen."

Mrs. Cragg cleared her throat. "Barnaby, please don't be rude." Then she turned to us. "Children, this is Barnaby Bratford, my boss."

PROFILE

Name: Barnaby Bratford

Age: Old enough to have warts on his fingers

Occupation: Owner of a babysitting company

Interests: Raising bullies

Mr. Bratford laughed—a wet, cough-y laugh. "Boss? Come now, I'm more than your boss. We're family!"

"Yes," Mrs. Cragg said, sounding almost ashamed. "Barnaby is my older brother."

Jeez. Now it made sense why Mrs. Cragg was so crabby all the time. Who'd want to be related to *that*?

Abby started barking and acting a bit jumpy, so I put her on the leash. Meanwhile, Mr. Bratford walked over to Mrs. Cragg's car.

"Do you have the paperwork?"

Mrs. Cragg nodded. "Yes, in the glove compartment."

I was confused. "What's he getting?" I asked.

"It's unfortunate that it didn't work out with Agnes and your family," Mr. Bratford said.

Her first name was *Agnes*? *Agnes Cragg?* Jeez, I was really starting to feel sorry for this lady.

Mr. Bratford pulled an envelope out of the car. "It's very important to match up the right babysitters with the right families. Unfortunately, this was not an ideal match." He held up the envelope. "This is Mrs. Cragg's evaluation of your family, so I can get right back to work providing a more suitable match for you next time. Well, good afternoon, everybody."

146

As he headed back to his van, Abby got even more jumpy.

"You have to control that dog," Mrs. Cragg whispered to me. But this time, it seemed like she was more worried than mad.

"I'm trying!" I said, but I was failing. Daisy tried to help, but she was no use; Abby dragged us all over to Mr. Bratford's van, where she started pawing at the door.

Mr. Bratford looked annoyed. "What is that mutt doing?" he snarled, trying to swat Abby away and open the van door at the same time.

"I'll make her stop," I said. The last thing I needed was for Abby to cause trouble with the head of the whole babysitting company.

I bent over and said "STOP!" in as firm a voice as I could. And Abby did stop—just long enough for me and Daisy to loosen our grip on her leash.

At which point she jumped through the window of the van, right into the front seat.

"NOT AGAIN!" I screamed. I tried to pull Abby out, but she was already tearing through something that was on the passenger seat.

"WHAT'S THAT DOG DOING?" Mr. Bratford hollered,

reaching into the van and trying to grab Abby's collar. But she hopped to the backseat and got away.

I looked through the window and noticed what she was digging into: an entire box of candy bars. It looked like she'd already eaten about three.

"Abby, you're going to get sick again!" I screamed. If she threw up in Mr. Bratford's car, she was going back to the shelter *for sure*.

Luckily, Mr. Bratford was able to grab Abby. She still had something in her mouth though, and as Mr. Bratford pulled her through the window, she dropped it right on top of the envelope he was holding.

It was half of a chocolate bar, still in its wrapper.

"Hey!" Mr. Bratford hollered, staring at his chocolate-covered envelope. He quickly grabbed the candy bar—wrapper and all—and threw it on the ground.

"You shouldn't litter," Daisy said.

"You shouldn't have a dog that steals," he said back.

I looked down at the wrapper. It looked just like the one that Abby found on our street after the car pulled away the night before.

Which had also been dropped on the ground by a litterer.

Wearing a striped shirt.

Hold on a second.

"Mr. Bratford, were you outside our house last night?" I asked.

"Of course not," he said, but I could tell he was lying.

"What were you doing there? And who was the other person you were with?"

"What's going on?" Daisy asked.

"I heard Mr. Bratford talking to someone outside my house," I told her. "He was asking that person to bring him something. Isn't that right, Mr. Bratford?"

He laughed. "As if I need to explain myself to a couple of children."

Mr. Bratford opened the door to his van, but before he could get in, Abby jumped up and started pawing at the envelope in his hands, which was still smeared with chocolate.

"Abby, you're being such a pig!" I yelled. "Stop it!"

I tried to yank her away, but Abby just started pawing harder.

"GET OFF ME!" yelled Mr. Bratford, trying to push Abby off—but as he swatted at her, the envelope fell to the ground.

Before anyone could react, Abby ripped open the envelope and started licking it all over. She was only interested in the chocolate, but the rest of us were staring at what had fallen out of the envelope.

It wasn't an evaluation, or even a piece of paper at all. It was something small and shiny. At first I couldn't tell what it was, but then I saw it glisten in the sunlight. It was a beautiful diamond necklace.

My mother's diamond necklace.

Her favorite diamond necklace. The one she'd worn two nights earlier. The one Mrs. Cragg had called "truly magnificent."

My heart started racing.

My blotch felt like it was going to explode.

I looked at Mrs. Cragg. She was making a face I'd never seen her make before. I couldn't quite figure it out at first. Then I realized what it was.

She was scared.

"Th-this isn't what it looks like," she stammered. "Your parents gave me the necklace, as a going-away present."

I stared at her. I realized exactly what was happening, and I suddenly felt totally calm. Like I was the one in control, for once.

Like Jonah Forrester. Like Hank Barlow. Like Daisy. Like Abby.

"I know what you two are," I said. "You're criminals. You're thieves. You stole my mother's necklace and you're going to go to jail."

"I can explain," whispered Mrs. Cragg, but it was clear she couldn't. She shrank backward and started crying.

"Oh, stop your sobbing," Mr. Bratford snarled at his sister. "Unless you're crying because you feel *bad*, because you ruined *everything*!" He was pacing like a caged animal.

"I'm sorry, Barnaby," she murmured.

Mr. Bratford bent down to put the necklace in his pocket, then turned to us. "It's a shame that you kids had to get caught in the middle of all this," he said. "I'm sure you understand, it's very important that none of you ever mention any of this to anyone. *Ever*. You have *no idea* what happened to the necklace. If you *ever* say *anything*, someone might get *hurt*."

Daisy and I stood there, frozen. Mr. Bratford reached for Abby.

"Now, about this dog here. I need to take her with me. I'm sure you understand."

"I *don't* understand, and you can't have her!" I said as Abby growled.

"Oh, don't you worry, I'll give her a good home."

"I don't believe you."

"These kids did nothing wrong!" Mrs. Cragg said. She looked at Abby. "And the dog is a little nuts, but—well, kind of cute."

"This is none of your concern." Mr. Bratford sneered at his sister.

Mr. Bratford was just about to grab Abby, when the next totally crazy thing happened.

"Enough!" Mrs. Cragg yelled. Then, without another word, Mrs. Cragg suddenly *ripped her own hair off her head*—that's right, I said *her own hair off her head*—and wrapped it around Mr. Bratford's eyes, like a blindfold.

"Your beautiful red hair!" I exclaimed. "It's a wig! Mrs. Cragg, you're bald!"

"Must be a family condition," Daisy explained. "Baxter's bald too."

FACT: There are a lot of great bald people in the world. But unfortunately, none of them are in this book.

"That's not important right now!" I said, which was the understatement of the year.

Meanwhile, Mr. Bratford was flailing around. "WHAT ARE YOU DOING?" he screamed at his sister.

"Run, kids!" Mrs. Cragg yelled. "Take Abby and run for your lives!"

And so, we did.

We ran for our lives.

Five seconds later, Mr. Bratford was running after us.

4:34 P.M.

DAISY, ABBY, AND I HAD BEEN SPRINTING FOR ABOUT THREE MINUTES BEFORE I REALIZED SOMETHING.

I had no idea where we were going. And neither did anyone else.

Meanwhile, we'd heard an engine start up, so we knew Barnaby Bratford was coming after us.

We stopped in the middle of the woods. All three of us were panting hard.

"My mom is going to be wondering where I am," Daisy said. "I told her I'd be home by four thirty." Then she looked at me and grinned. "Oh well."

I looked at her. "Aren't you even scared at all?"

"Of course I am!" she said. "I'm really scared. But also, this is the most excitement I've had in a long time." She bent down to scratch Abby's ears. "Besides, Abby's here, and she'll protect us, won't you, girl?"

I looked at the two of them and suddenly felt better. Why should I be scared? I had people (and a dog) who cared about me and would protect me. And I would protect them. We would protect each other.

It's like Jonah Forrester always says: *Some things are worth fighting for.* That was the line I always said from the roof at—

Wait a second.

That's it!

"I know where we can go," I told Daisy and Abby. They both looked at me.

"Out here, in the middle of nowhere?" Daisy asked.

"There's an old abandoned beach club on the other side of the swamp, called the Boathouse," I said. "It's a neat place to hang out."

"Cool!" Daisy said. Then she scratched her head. "But what will we do there?"

"There's a roof-deck. We can hide there until they give up looking for us. Then we go home and call the police."

Abby, meanwhile, had spotted a squirrel and suddenly yanked so hard on the leash that my arm almost came off.

"I see what you mean about Abby," Daisy said. "If she

hadn't spotted that box of candy bars, we never would have found out about the diamond necklace. That was awesome."

"Abby's awesome in general," I said. "Super awesome." Then, before I could stop myself, I added, "And you're awesome too."

Daisy smiled at me. I smiled at her. It was super-duper-duper awesome.

Then I remembered there was someone out there who wasn't awesome *at all*. And he was looking for us.

"We should probably go," I said, feeling like an actual leader all of a sudden.

"Okay," Daisy said, nodding. "Which way?"

"I know a dirt road. It will get us there faster."

She frowned. "Don't we want to stay off the roads though?"

"Trust me—no one even knows about it."

We cut through an old picnic area that still had a few broken-down old tables sitting there like they were begging for people to use them.

"See?" I said, grinning, as we turned onto the dirt road. It had so many vines and bushes growing over it that I didn't think any car could get down it anyway.

"You were right," Daisy agreed.

I was feeling really good about myself—*really* good—when I heard it.

A car engine.

Getting closer.

"RUN!" I yelled, but it was too late. The van came screeching up. Mr. Bratford had spotted us.

"THAT'S ENOUGH!" he yelled. I glanced back and saw him get out of his van and come sprinting full speed after us.

"Keep going!" I said to Daisy and Abby both. "We're almost there!" I tried to sound brave, but I knew that I'd made a big mistake by suggesting we take the dirt road. I'd gotten overconfident and careless.

Hank Barlow or Jonah Forrester would never have let that happen.

We scrambled up one hill, down another, and then there it was—the Boathouse, looking as empty and deserted as ever.

"Go around to the other side," I gasped, out of breath. "We'll go in the back way."

Abby had been there before, so she knew exactly where to go. We used an old rusted-out canoe to climb up onto the porch.

"The stairs are over there," I yelled. Abby and I ran ahead and Daisy followed. We turned the corner and suddenly heard a voice coming from the roof-deck.

"Uh-oh," Daisy whispered. "He must have gotten here first."

We crept closer until we could make out the words.

"HELLO OUT THERE! IT'S ME, KING OF THE WORLD!"

Wait a second, I said to myself. *I know that voice.*

"Irwin!?!?" I called. "Is that you?"

I heard a scuffling above me, and sure enough, Irwin peered down from the roof. "Jimmy?"

"What are you doing here?" I asked.

"This is my hiding place too," he answered, sounding a little annoyed. "What are *you* doing here? And why are you so out of breath?"

"It's a long story," I said.

"Is Daisy with you?" Irwin asked, of course.

"I'm here!" she called.

That's all it took. "I'll be down in a sec!" he said.

"No!" I said. "We're coming up there! We need to hide!"

But Irwin was already scrambling down. "Hide?" he said, jumping off the last step. "From who?"

"From me, I believe," said a voice behind us. We all

turned around and there he was: Barnaby Bratford, stepping onto the porch, drumming his pimply fingers together. Mrs. Cragg was next to him, bald as a cue ball, looking like she'd have rather been anywhere else.

"Nice place you got here," Mr. Bratford went on. "A fixer-upper, I see."

"Who are you?" Irwin said.

"Oh, I'm the dog warden," answered Mr. Bratford. "I've come for this adorable girl here. Want to hand her over?"

I picked Abby up. She was heavy, but I pretended not to notice. I saw her fangs peeking out. I petted her fur slowly, trying to keep her calm. It was like she was waiting for the right time to pounce. I was praying there would be one.

"Abby is awesome, and I'm taking her home," I told Mr. Bratford, as if I were talking to a normal person. "My parents are going to wonder where I am, so we should probably go."

Mr. Bratford's big sweaty hand patted the top of my head. "Well, here's the problem with that," he said. "I'm not so sure that's true. From what Agnes tells me, your parents aren't all that worried about what you're up to. Your mom works all the time, and your dad's running around looking for a job. Who has time for unimportant things like children?" He stuck his face right down in front of mine, close enough so I could smell the pickles he had for lunch. "That's where my fine babysitting service comes in!"

I heard a small, soft growl from Abby.

"Shhh, it's going to be okay," I whispered to her, even though I was starting to worry that maybe it wasn't. "You're not taking her anywhere," I told Mr. Bratford.

Mr. Bratford nodded, smiling. "Oooh, feisty." He pinched my cheek so hard that tears came to my eyes, then put one of his pimply hands on Abby and started petting her fur.

"Get your hands off her," I said evenly.

FACT: Sometimes bravery isn't exactly bravery. Sometimes it's more like stupidity.

The next thing I knew, Mr. Bratford had picked me up by the shirt and was carrying me over to Mrs. Cragg.

"Please keep an eye on him," he told her.

"I didn't mean for any of this to happen," Mrs. Cragg whispered to me. "Abby was supposed to stay home! I'm really sorry."

"A little too late for that," I told her. But she looked really upset, so I added, "It's not all your fault."

Mr. Bratford pointed at Daisy and Irwin. "Have a

seat, you two." They sat down on the old couch by the
rusted-out fireplace. Mr. Bratford began pacing back and
forth.

"Well," said Mr. Bratford, "I suppose that you have
a right to know why I need to take your dog. It seems
only fair."

I could tell by his evil grin that fairness had nothing
to do with it. He just wanted to make us squirm.

"You see," he went on, "knowledge can be a dangerous
thing. And the problem is, you and your blotchy little
face and your silly little friends and your ratty little dog
know too much." Mr. Bratford patted Daisy and Irwin on
their heads. "Now, of course, I would never do anything

to hurt you beautiful children," he said. "That would be extremely stupid of me. I have a business to run, after all." Then he turned and looked at Abby. "Unfortunately, this poor little pooch here won't be quite so lucky." He grabbed Mrs. Cragg's cane out of her hand and started using it as a walking stick. "Here's the story we're going with: there was a terrible accident. It turns out your dog chewed up your mother's jewelry case, grabbed the necklace, and ran away. You chased her all the way to this place, and as you tried to grab her, the dog fell tragically off the roof to her death—both dog and necklace lost forever into the swamp below."

"Please don't hurt the dog," Mrs. Cragg whimpered.

"Quiet!" Mr. Bratford thundered at his sister. "We had it all worked out. The dog was a gift! A perfect excuse for you to quit that job, *and* a perfect explanation for why the necklace went missing. Dogs destroy, lose, or bury things all the time, don't they? It was a foolproof plan! And you had to go and ruin it by bringing that crazy dog with you today!"

"That's actually a stupid plan," Daisy said. "No one would have ever believed that."

"They wouldn't even try a plot like that on *STOP! POLICE!*" Irwin added, probably for my benefit.

"Oh, I used to love that show as a kid," Mr. Bratford said. "I always wanted Hank Barlow to die though, and he never did."

"You're a horrible human being," I told him.

"Perhaps," said Barnaby Bratford, "but I'm a *rich* horrible human being. And if any of you children ever say one word about what *really* happened here today, you will follow that dog into the swamp."

I closed my eyes and opened them, hoping it was all a nightmare. It wasn't. "You are going to pay for this!" I yelled.

"Ah, but again, that's where you're wrong," Mr. Bratford said. "I'm going to *get paid* for this."

He started walking toward me. I was still holding Abby, and my arms were getting really tired. She started growling again.

"Give me that dog," Mr. Bratford said.

"Shhhh," I whispered to Abby. "Everything will be okay."

Abby growled louder as Mr. Bratford got closer.

"HAND HER OVER!" he screamed.

That's when Abby decided to make her move.

In one split second, she jumped out of my arms, bared

her teeth, leaped onto Mr. Bratford, and clamped her jaws around his neck.

Mr. Bratford screamed and fell down. Abby clamped harder, and they started rolling around on the ground.

"THIS DOG'S INSANE!" screamed Mr. Bratford as he started flailing furiously at Abby.

"She's not insane," I said. "She's a crime-fighting vampire dog!"

FACT: Sometimes it's better to just come right out and say it.

"A crime-fighting vampire dog, ha!" Mr. Bratford gasped. Then he grabbed Mrs. Cragg's cane and whacked Abby right on the nose. Abby yelped in pain and let go of Mr. Bratford, who scrambled to his feet.

"AHA!" he screamed, panting. "Would a crime-fighting vampire dog cry and moan like that from one little poke? I don't think so." Mr. Bratford took out his phone and shoved it in my face. "Look!" he wheezed. There was a picture of a dog with a very fancy haircut. "My dog is better than your dog! My dog is a thoroughbred Akita bred from a long line of show champions, and your dog is nothing more than a filthy mangy mutt!"

Abby was shivering and whimpering. I think she was in shock. We both were.

I bent down and kissed the top of her head. "Are you okay, girl?" I asked.

She responded by licking me on the face.

Right on my blotch.

FACT: Ordinarily, getting your blotch licked by a dog would be gross. But not in this case. Definitely not in this case.

Here's what happened after Abby licked my blotch:

The fur on her head tickled my nose and made me sneeze.

The sneeze went right in Mr. Bratford's face.

Mr. Bratford yelled, "That's disgusting!" and furiously wiped his face with his hands.

Which made him drop Mrs. Cragg's cane.

Which dropped next to my hand.

Which I picked up and used to whack Mr. Bratford's knee.

"AAARRRRGH!!!" he yelled.

"YOU CAN SAY THAT AGAIN!" I yelled. Then I smacked his other knee, and sure enough, he screamed "AAARRRRGH!!!" again.

He fell to the ground, which gave us a few seconds to try and figure out our next move.

"Let's go up to the roof," Irwin said.

Daisy looked confused. "Huh?"

"The roof?" I said. "Why would we do that? We'll get trapped up there."

"Trust me!" Irwin said.

"But why?" I said.

Irwin stared at me. "Because I'm your best friend, that's why."

Mr. Bratford, meanwhile, was back on his feet. "I've had it, you little brats," he said, wheezing. "Enough is enough."

"I'm going to head up to the roof and call for help!" Irwin yelled. "There's a house across the swamp, they'll be able to see us if we're on the roof!"

I still had no idea what he was up to. There wasn't a house anywhere near us.

"Come up to the roof, Jimmy," he begged.

Mr. Bratford started limping toward me.

I looked at Irwin. His eyes were flickering back and forth, from me to the stairs. I tried to figure out his plan, but I couldn't.

"Would you please come up to the roof?" Irwin said to

me, overemphasizing the word *would*. "WOULD you? WOULD you? WOULD you?"

I had no idea what he was talking about—

Until I did.

Would.

As in, *wood.*

"I got it!" I shouted. "Daisy, Abby, come on!"

"Got what?" Mr. Bratford gasped.

We didn't answer—instead, Daisy, Irwin, Abby, and I ran to the stairs and charged up to the roof, with Mr. Bratford on our heels.

"Do you guys know what you're doing?" Daisy asked.

We both nodded.

Five seconds later, Mr. Bratford made it up. He looked around. "Come now. Why would you kids try to trick an adult?" He looked at me. "Now give me that dog, and this will all be over."

"I will never give you this dog," I said, backing up.

"You're getting awfully close to the edge," Mr. Bratford said. "Give me that dog NOW."

I refused to look behind me, because I was totally afraid of heights. "If Abby goes over the roof," I managed to say, "then I'm going too."

Mr. Bratford sighed. "Well, I must say I'm impressed, Swimmy Jimmy. Baxter always told me you were a loser. But it turns out you've got some fight in you! Good for you. However, there's a point when fighting becomes useless. And I'm afraid we've reached that point."

I knew that the edge of the roof was getting closer. In another five feet, I would be toast.

FACT: There are two kinds of toast. There's the good kind, with butter and sugar and cinnamon. And then there's the bad kind.

I stopped backing up. Meanwhile, Irwin and Abby had moved to the other side of the roof, next to the hot tub. Irwin nodded at me—it was now or never.

I put Abby down.

"Run to Irwin and Daisy!" I said.

Abby didn't move. I think she wanted to stay and protect me.

"Go!" I urged—but still nothing.

"I've got you now!" Mr. Bratford said gleefully. He reached out to grab her, but she slithered out of his grasp.

Which is when Irwin yelled, "SOME THINGS ARE WORTH FIGHTING FOR . . . BUT JUSTICE IS WORTH BITING FOR!"

I couldn't believe it. Irwin was quoting Jonah Forrester—and it worked! Abby started running, and then she jumped.

And when I say jumped, I mean . . . she JUMPED.

She soared over Mr. Bratford, and over half the roof, toward Irwin. She was in the air so long, it seemed like the black stripe of fur along her back was acting as a cape.

So she wasn't just a crime-fighting vampire dog.

She was a *superhero* crime-fighting vampire dog.

As she flew by Mr. Bratford, he tried to grab her, taking two steps backward.

Right onto the rotted plank of wood by the chimney.

Which broke.

"AAAAAAAAAHHHHH!" Mr. Bratford screamed, as he fell through the brand-new hole in the roof to the floor below.

Then: *CRAAAAAAASHHHH!*

Mrs. Cragg was still down there, waiting for it to all be over. She screamed, "BARNABY!" then asked, "Are you all right?!?!"

The only answer was a long, painful moan.

"You might want to give him some kelp," I called down to Mrs. Cragg.

Daisy and Irwin ran over to me, and we all hugged. "We did it!" I said, over and over again. "We did it!" Meanwhile, Abby was squealing with joy and giving me tons of kisses.

"I'm so glad you're okay," Daisy told me.

"You're not as glad as I am," Irwin told her, needing the last word, as always. But this time, instead of being irritated, I just laughed.

"You were worried about me?" I asked Irwin.

"Of course I was worried about you," Irwin said. "You're my best friend."

"You're my best friend too," I told him.

We went down the stairs. Mr. Bratford was lying there with two hurt knees and bruises all over his body, cursing and howling. Mrs. Cragg, meanwhile, was calling 911.

I leaned down right next to the pimply-fingered crook who tried to take my mom's necklace—not to mention Abby.

"*My* dog is better than *your* dog," I whispered in his ear, "and don't you ever forget it."

6:16 P.M.

FIVE MINUTES LATER, the place was crawling with police cars and ambulances.

It was exactly like an episode of *STOP! POLICE!*

Mr. Bratford was placed on a stretcher and put into an ambulance. Believe it or not, he was still insulting me up until the last second. "Might want to get that looked at," he said, pointing at my blotch.

"And you might want to find out what kind of food they serve in jail," I shot back.

Mrs. Cragg, who was still clutching her red wig, was put in a police car. She looked shocked, terrified, and relieved, all at the same time.

"Good luck," I heard myself say, as her car drove away, but I don't think she heard me.

I waved to Daisy and Irwin as they got in a different police car.

"Where are they going?" I asked an officer.

"They're going home so their parents can take them to the police station," the police officer said—which made me suddenly feel bad that both of my parents were far away, in the city.

The officer put her hand on my shoulder. "Your folks are on their way too," she said. "Hopefully they'll be at the station by the time we get there."

"Thanks," I said.

Abby and I climbed into the back of the officer's police car. I stared at the Boathouse as we drove away. I still couldn't believe what had happened. It was the most exciting, intense, and scary thing that had ever happened to me.

And exhausting too, I guess—because then I fell asleep.

"WAKE UP, KID. WE'RE HERE."

"Huh? Where are we? What happened?"

"Well, you've had quite a day, that's what happened."

I rubbed my eyes. Abby was next to me. Slowly, it all came back to me. Mrs. Cragg. Barnaby Bratford. The Boathouse.

Irwin and Daisy. Abby and me.

I sat up, got out of the car, and looked around. We were at the police station.

"Is Mr. Bratford going to be in a lot of trouble?"

"He sure is," said the police officer. "We've had detectives working on this case for a while. There's been a series of jewelry thefts in town, and they were just starting to tie them back to the Bratford babysitting service. The only thing missing was hard evidence, but now, thanks to you and your pals, we have it. This guy's going to jail for a long, long time. His sister too."

"It wasn't all Mrs. Cragg's fault," I heard myself saying. "He made her do it. She tried to help us in the end."

The police officer looked surprised. "Well, she'll get her day in court." She nodded at Abby. "That's a pretty darn cute dog you got there, by the way."

"She's more than cute." I looked at Abby and smiled. I'm pretty sure she smiled back.

The officer pointed and smiled too. "In the meantime, there are some people here who'd really like to see you."

I looked and saw my parents and Misty, standing inside the police station with scared looks on their faces. I have to admit I kind of liked seeing them all worried about me, and part of me wanted to let them worry just a few seconds more. But it was only a small part of me, so I started walking toward them. Then I started running, and when they saw me, they ran too.

When we reached each other, we all fell into a big, long group hug.

"Hey," I said.

My mom was too busy crying to hug me. My dad's face broke into a huge smile of relief as he picked me up in his arms. "Jimmy," he said, over and over. "Jimmy. Jimmy. Jimmy."

"Did you get the job?" I asked him.

My dad laughed. "You are something else," he said.

Finally, he put me down. Then Misty came over and hugged me again, really hard. She was crying too. I wasn't sure I'd ever seen her cry before, except for that one time that she wanted to move to Paris by herself for her twelfth birthday and my dad said no.

"I hate you," she whispered.

"I hate you more," I whispered back.

But neither of us meant it.

8:31 P.M.

LATER THAT NIGHT, AFTER WE WERE FINALLY ABLE TO LEAVE THE POLICE STATION, we had an amazing dinner: fried chicken, applesauce, fresh corn, and my mom's special rice (tons of butter).

There wasn't a fried beet or garlic muffin in sight.

"That was delicious!" I said, wiping my mouth. "What's for dessert?"

"We're going out for ice cream," my dad said.

Misty and I high-fived. Abby wagged her tail.

"Before we go, I want to say something," my mom said. "I know things have been crazy around the house. I work a lot, and your dad's been trying to find a job, and maybe it seems that we've been ignoring you guys a little bit." She stopped talking for a second, wiped a tear from her eye, then continued. "I guess that sometimes, we forget what the two most important things in our lives are."

I was confused. "Which are what?"

Misty smacked me on the arm. "Us, you dummy!"

"Oh," I said, rubbing my arm. "And also, ouch."

My dad laughed but then turned serious again. "So, about that job thing: I'm going to take it, but only part-time. I do want to go back to work full-time at some point—it's only fair that you know that—but for now, it's important that I be here when you guys get home from school."

"No more babysitters for the time being," added my mom.

I breathed a sigh of relief.

"Stop using the word *babysitter*," Misty said. "It makes me sound like I'm five years old."

"Would you prefer chauffeur?" asked my dad.

Misty snickered. "Definitely." Then for some annoying reason, she put me in a headlock. "Now that we're one big happy family again, can we go get that ice cream?"

"Wait," I said, untangling myself from her grip. "I want to say something too. It's about Abby."

"We're keeping her, honey," my mom said. "Of course we're keeping her."

"It's not that." I bent down to scratch Abby's ears. "It's

just . . . I think there's something you should know about her—"

Abby suddenly started jumping up and down, barking wildly.

"What's going on?" asked Misty. "What's she barking at? Is it a deer? Another burglar?"

I looked out the front window but didn't see anything. Then I looked out the back window but didn't see anything there either. For some reason though, Abby kept barking and barking.

"What were you going to tell us about Abby?" yelled my dad, over the barking. "Other than she's going to make us all deaf?"

I tried to talk, but Abby kept barking and barking.

Then, finally, I got it. I understood why she was barking.

She didn't want me to say anything.

She wanted her secret powers to stay secret.

PART FOUR

THE REST OF THE STORY

FRIDAY, AUGUST 29

7:07 A.M.

FOR SOME REASON, WHEN I WOKE UP THE NEXT MORNING, I thought my blotch might be gone.

Wrong.

Here's the good news though: the ointment my mom got me was working. It was no longer the size of Alaska, or even California or Texas, the three biggest states in the country. It was more like Nebraska.

I could live with Nebraska.

When I went downstairs to get some cereal before school, everyone was there. Mom was still home, even though it was after seven. Misty was sitting on the counter, texting somebody. And for some reason, Dad was making a huge breakfast. Eggs, bacon, juice—everything.

"Dad, what's with the spread?" Misty said.

"You know it's a school day, right?" I added. "We're kind of in a rush."

"School day, schmool day," he answered. "I'm making breakfast for my family." He put a plate in front of me. "Dig in!"

I tried to look excited. "Great!"

FACT: My dad's eggs taste worse than boiled kelp.

I took one bite, tried not to gag, and wolfed down a bowl of Super Sugar Flakies. Then I grabbed my backpack. "Well, don't want to be late for school," I said.

I was halfway out the door before I felt my mom's hand on my shoulder. I turned back and she gave me a long, strong, warm hug. It felt really good.

"Have a good day at work, Mom," I said. But she wasn't letting go.

"I feel like what happened was my fault," she whispered.

"It wasn't," I said. "It wasn't anyone's fault, except Barnaby Bratford's."

She smiled at me, and I could tell she was crying a little.

"How did I get such a great kid?"

"Just lucky, I guess."

She gave me one last squeeze.

"I'd take you over Hank Barlow any day," she said.

10:47 A.M.

"THAT WAS SO GROSS WHEN SHE LICKED YOUR BLOTCH," IRWIN SAID.

"It kind of was," Daisy agreed.

We were at recess, going over the whole thing for about the sixty-second time. All the other kids who'd listened the first sixty-one times had drifted away—but we were still going at it.

"Don't you guys get it?" I said. "When she licked my blotch, all these amazing things happened. It ended up saving our lives, practically." I leaned my blotch toward Irwin's face. "Do you want to give it a lick and see?"

Irwin looked like he was about to throw up. "Ugh! I'm not getting anywhere near that thing!"

"I may as well tell you guys," I said. "I'm pretty sure Abby has secret powers."

"Here we go again," Irwin said.

"I'm serious," I said. "Like, she's a vampire. And a superhero. And a crime fighter." They were looking at me like I was crazy, but there was no turning back now. "A superhero crime-fighting vampire dog. She has all these powers that she uses for the good of mankind. Just like Jonah Forrester. And Hank Barlow. Except she's a dog."

Irwin started laughing uncontrollably, but Daisy managed to look like she was trying to believe me. "What makes you think that?" she asked.

"Did you see how far she jumped from me to you guys on the roof? That wasn't jumping—that was flying!"

"I've seen other dogs jump that far," Irwin said.

"Well, she sleeps all day," I said.

Irwin stopped laughing long enough to sputter, "Most dogs sleep all day."

I rattled off the list of Abby's vampire habits, but Irwin had an answer for every one.

Me: "She hates the light."

Him: "You told me she has something wrong with her eyes."

Me: "She sneaks out of the house in the middle of the night."

Him: "You might have dreamed that."

Me: "I saw her bite one person and almost bite another!"

Him: "Dogs bite, especially when threatened. That's what they do."

Me: "But only Abby bites to fight crime."

Irwin thought for a minute, then said, "So what you're saying is that Abby isn't a crime fighter, she's a crime-*biter*." He started cracking up again, while Daisy and Irwin started chanting, "Crimebiter! Crimebiter! Abby the crimebiting dog!"

That made me mad—and desperate.

Me: "She likes chocolate, which looks a lot like blood."

Him, rolling his eyes: "Fail. Total fail."

Finally, I lost my patience and yelled, "ABBY IS A SUPERHERO CRIME-FIGHTING VAMPIRE DOG AND I DON'T CARE WHAT YOU SAY!"

Irwin and Daisy stopped laughing long enough to give each other the *I think he's a little crazy* look.

"How about this," Daisy said. "How about the fact that before you got Abby, you were kind of shy, you kept to yourself and spent most of your time watching old episodes of *STOP! POLICE!* and reading the same vampire books over and over, and now, you've been through an incredible adventure and stopped a horrible criminal and were a really brave hero." She smiled. "So maybe *that's* Abby's secret power."

"I suppose that could be true," I said, even though I wasn't convinced.

"Hey, I have an idea," Irwin said. "If she has special powers, why don't you ask her to remove that thing on your face?"

I immediately touched my blotch. It was still there, red and warm.

"I think your mark gives your face some real character," Daisy said.

I felt myself starting to blush, which made the blotch get even hotter. "What do you mean?"

Daisy lightly touched my blotch with her finger. I stopped blushing. I may have even stopped breathing. "I mean," she said, "it makes you seem like you're an interesting person who lives an interesting life."

Irwin snorted. "Well, you definitely led an interesting last couple of days," he said, "but it didn't have anything to do with a superhero crime-fighting vampire dog."

I was about to get mad at him but then I remembered he'd helped save my dog's life.

FACT: If someone saves your dog's life, you're not allowed to get mad at them ever again, no matter how many annoying things they say.

Suddenly, there was a lot of noise over by the jungle gym. A bad feeling came over me—it was the same exact place where Baxter Bratford had made fun of me and my blotch the day before.

But a lot had happened since then, including his dad getting arrested.

As the three of us ran over to see what was going on, I heard yelling.

"Your dad's a crook!" someone screamed.

"He tried to kill a dog!" someone else yelled. "Are you going to try and kill a dog too?"

Then I saw Baxter, sitting by himself on a swing.

They were screaming and yelling at him.

This time, *he* was the one being bullied.

"I'm surprised he's in school today," Irwin said.

Daisy sighed sadly. "I heard it's like a circus at his house, with a ton of news reporters and stuff, so I guess he's better off here than there."

I wasn't sure what to do. Baxter had made my life miserable for a long, long time, and his dad had tried to kill my dog, but for some reason, I didn't want to join in.

In fact, I wanted to do just the opposite.

"That's enough, you guys!" I yelled. "Stop it."

Everyone stopped and looked at me, shocked. I guess they figured I would be more excited than anybody to give Baxter a taste of his own medicine.

"I mean it," I continued. "Leave Baxter alone. It's not his fault his dad is a bad person." Then I looked at him. "Just like it's not my fault I have a mark on my face."

Baxter got up off the swing and walked over to me. "I didn't mean any of that stuff I did to you," he said. "I guess I was just a real jerk because somehow I knew my dad was a jerk too. It made me mad all the time, and I took it out on you." He looked like he was about to cry. "I'm really sorry."

He stuck his hand out. I shook it.

"Thank you for saying sorry," I told him. "And you know what? I get mad sometimes too. I get mad at my mom for working all the time. And I just got mad at my dad for wanting to find a job so he didn't have to take care of us anymore. But that doesn't make it okay to be mean to other people."

Daisy and Irwin walked up to us. Irwin looked a little nervous, but Daisy went right up to Baxter and put her hand on his shoulder.

"Do you maybe want to eat lunch with us?" she asked.

Baxter smiled, and I realized it was the first time I'd ever seen him look truly happy.

"I'd like that," he said. "I'd like that a lot."

And the four of us went inside.

6:49 P.M.

SINCE IT WAS FRIDAY NIGHT—AND IT HAD BEEN, IN MY
DAD'S WORDS, "A HECKUVA WEEK"—I WAS ALLOWED TO
HAVE IRWIN SLEEP OVER. Daisy came too, but she wasn't
allowed to sleep over, since she was a girl.

At dinner, there was a big package on my plate.

"For me?" I said.

"For you," my mom said.

I ripped it open. Inside were two things: the entire
Jonah Forrester series of four Fang books, and the first
season of *STOP! POLICE!* on DVD.

"We still think you spend too much time with this
stuff," said my dad, "but if you have to spend too much
time with something, it might as well be something
worthwhile, right?"

I hugged my parents as Irwin and Daisy giggled.

"Are there any episodes in *STOP! POLICE!* about a

vampire dog?" asked Irwin. "Does Hank have a pet vampire?" I shot him a look though, and he stopped.

After dinner, I talked Irwin and Daisy into watching the movie version of *Fang You Very Much*, which was like a prequel to *Fang Goodness*. In the plot, Jonah Forrester is a science whiz in high school, until an experiment goes horribly wrong and changes him forever. The movie ends with him sneaking out of his house through a window in the middle of the night and starting his new life as a vampire.

We had just started the movie when my mom came into the room.

"I just got a call from Baxter's mom," she said. "She's really worried about him. I guess there's still a ton of reporters and cameras staked out around their house and he feels trapped and lonely. And he said to his mom that the only people he'd actually want to see are you guys, because you all said you'd be his friend. Is that true?"

"Yup," I said.

My mom thought for a second. "Well, it might be nice to invite him over tonight."

I suddenly got a little nervous. "Tonight? Like, to sleep over?"

My dad walked into the room. "We'll see about

sleeping over," he said. "But I know one thing: I bet he could really stand to get out of that house right about now."

Irwin, Daisy, and I looked at each other.

Finally, Daisy cleared her throat. "I think it would be really nice if he came over," she said. Then she looked at me. "If it's okay with you," she added.

I thought for a second. "It's okay with me."

Twenty minutes later, the doorbell rang. Baxter and his mother were standing there.

"We had to sneak out the back of our house," he told me. "Thank you for letting me come over."

"I'm glad you came," I said.

While Baxter was saying hi to Daisy and Irwin, his mom came up to me. She was small and skinny and looked like she hadn't slept in two years. "I just want to say to you . . ." She couldn't finish what she was saying, because she started crying. But it didn't matter, because I knew what she was trying to say.

"It's okay," I said to her.

"Thank you," she whispered.

I looked over at Baxter. "We're watching a movie," I told him. "Do you want to watch it with us?"

"Are you sure it's okay?" he asked.

I grinned. "Just don't hog the popcorn."

We restarted the movie, and it was just getting to the good part—the part when Jonah is about to become a vampire—when I blurted out something I'd been thinking about for a while.

"I think we should form a gang," I said.

They all looked at me.

"I think we should form a gang, and we need a name," I added. "How about CrimeBiters?"

Irwin put the movie on pause. "You got all mad today at school when we called Abby a crimebiter."

I stood up and went to stand by Abby, who was at the window, watching the neighborhood, on high alert. "I know, but I like it now. It sounds cool. I think it would make a good name for a gang. CrimeBiters."

"It would," agree Daisy. "The only problem is, I'm not sure we need to form a gang to fight crime."

"Yeah," Irwin said, stuffing his face with popcorn. "Personally, I'm good with a gang that hangs out and watches movies and stuff."

"Why do you say that?" I asked.

"Because nothing bad ever really happens around here," answered Irwin. "Most people are totally normal, except for a few bad guys." Then he looked at Baxter. "Sorry."

"That's okay," Baxter said, but you could tell he felt anything but okay.

"What's going to happen to Mrs. Cragg?" I asked. "I can't believe I'm saying this, but I feel sort of sorry for her."

"Thanks," Baxter said, trying to smile. "My mom thinks if she admits everything and testifies in court, there's a chance she'll only get probation and community service."

"That's great," I said. "As long as she never, ever cooks fried beets in pea sauce again."

We all laughed, and I realized my friends were right. Our town was basically pretty quiet. Definitely no real need for an amateur team of crime fighters.

I pointed at Abby. "Well, I'm glad she's here to keep an eye on things," I told my friends. "Because you never know."

"You watch too many crime shows on TV," Irwin said.

Daisy and Baxter nodded in agreement with Irwin.

"Let's get dessert," I suggested.

FACT: Ice cream is an amazing way to change the subject.

As we piled into the kitchen, Misty pulled me aside. "What were you guys talking about in there?" she asked.

I smiled and shook my head. "Just friend stuff," I said, throwing her favorite answer back at her.

She laughed. "Just friend stuff. Excellent. You're learning."

A minute later, my parents poked their heads in.

"Sorry to break up the party, but Daisy's mom called and wants her home," my mom said. "And as for the rest of you, it's bedtime."

"After our ice cream sodas!" I whined.

"Okay, fine," said my dad. "But then, everyone upstairs!"

Five minutes later, we said good-bye to Daisy. As we watched her walk across the street to her house, Irwin turned to me.

"Sorry, dude, but I think she likes me," he said.

"Not a chance," I said. "She likes *me*."

We both looked at Baxter.

"Leave me out of it," he said.

FACT: If two friends are fighting over a girl and ask your opinion on who's right, the only way to stay friends with both of them is to keep your mouth shut.

While we brushed our teeth, I took one last look in the mirror. My blotch was back down to the size it was when I first discovered it three days earlier—the shape of Rhode Island, according to my dad. The medicine was definitely working. Did that mean it was going away for good? I had a weird thought all of a sudden.

I wasn't sure I wanted it to *totally* go away. It seemed to bring me luck, in a strange sort of way.

And besides, Daisy said it gave me "character."

Back in my room, we all got in our sleeping bags. Abby came in and climbed all over us, nipping and pawing.

"See how playful she is at night?" I said to the guys. "That's another sign that she—"

"Let it go," Irwin said. "Let it go."

It was obvious I couldn't convince him.

Yet.

10:24 P.M.

It was a lonely life, yes, but a noble one. Jonah couldn't get close enough to anyone to reveal his true self, but it was a price he was willing to pay. He had no choice. He was there to help people, whether they knew who he was or not. It was part of the deal. Yes, he was alone. Yes, he could get discouraged. But he couldn't have been more proud of who he was. And no one could take that away from him . . .

IRWIN AND BAXTER HAD DRIFTED OFF TO SLEEP, BUT I STAYED AWAKE, reading the last few pages of *Fang Goodness.*

Eventually, I closed the book, then closed my eyes and thought about the book. *This is totally made up,* I said to myself. *None of this could ever actually happen. Right?* I watched Abby in the closet, playing with a sock, and I tried to see Irwin's side. Maybe I *was* being dumb. Maybe

I *was* letting my imagination run away with me. Maybe it *was* just a coincidence that Abby had eyes that were really sensitive to light and a tendency to bite bad guys on the neck. I laughed, thinking how silly it must have sounded to my friends . . . me thinking that she was anything other than a regular dog with a few strange habits . . . *Grow up, Jimmy,* I said to myself. *It's not possible . . . It's not . . . It's . . .*

Whoosh! Thwack!

I woke up with a jump. There was Abby, right on schedule, tiptoeing along the windowsill. I wanted to wake up the other guys, but then I decided not to. Maybe it was better this way.

Maybe it was good that I was the only one who knew what Abby really was.

In a flash, she darted through the open window, leaped to the lawn below and started walking in circles, sniffing and panting.

I watched her and wondered: *Maybe she's just out there looking for groundhogs.*

But maybe not.

Maybe Abby was working.

Because after all . . . a CrimeBiter's job is never done.

ACKNOWLEDGMENTS

A HUGE FANG YOU to my incomparable editor, Nancy Mercado, for keeping a straight face when I pitched her an idea about a vampire dog; to David Levithan, Yaffa Jaskoll, Rachael Hicks, Erica Ferguson, Jeremy West, and the whole team at Scholastic Press for their wonderful Scholasticness; to Adam Stower for creating drawings that made me laugh out loud; and to the swell Brianne Johnson, for telling me what to sign, why to sign, when to sign, and most importantly, where to sign.

ABOUT THE AUTHOR

TOMMY GREENWALD AND HIS DOG, ABBY

Photo credit: Suzanne Sheridan

TOMMY GREENWALD is the author of the Charlie Joe Jackson series about the most reluctant reader ever born. Tommy lives in Connecticut with his wife, Cathy; their kids, Charlie, Joe, and Jack; and their dogs, Coco and Abby. Abby is not necessarily a crime-fighting vampire dog—but she makes Tommy and his family very, very happy, which is definitely a kind of superpower when you think about it.